The Short Ones

are the Best

The Short Ones are the Best

John Worthington

First published in Great Britain in 2017 by

Bannister Publications Ltd
118 Saltergate
Chesterfield
Derbyshire S40 1NG

Copyright © John Worthington

ISBN 978-1-909813-39-7

John Worthington asserts the moral right to be identified
as the author of this work

A catalogue record for this book is available from the British Library

Typeset by Escritor Design, Bournemouth

Printed and bound in Great Britain

www.bannisterpublications.com

I wish to express my thanks and gratitude to my wife Pam, who kept me fed and watered throughout my writing of this book, and not forgetting Sarah, without whose guidance, the end product would not have been achieved.

And also, to all those unnamed members of the public, who through their innocent conversations helped me to inject a little humour into some of the storylines.

Contents

A Strange but True Story
that happened to the Author

BEFORE I BEGIN to tell this story it is important to explain, that prior to these happenings I had never before been to an airport or travelled by aeroplane. The year was 1966, and my wife Pam and I, along with our two children - Tracy and Adrian, had begun to make plans to emigrate to Canada. The chosen destination in Canada was to be Edmonton, Alberta.

The Canadian Immigration Authority had, at that time, strict rules in place that as the breadwinner, only I was initially able to enter Canada as an immigrant. And until such time that I had found employment with sufficient earnings to support my family, Pam and our children would not be allowed to join me.

Approximately four to six months before my departure to Canada, which was to be May 1967, I had a dream one night which I have never disclosed to anyone. I dreamt that I was in an airport awaiting the arrival of my family from England. I was accompanied by a work colleague who had kindly driven me out to the airport. In this dream my family's flight was due to arrive that evening, but then it was announced over the public address system that the flight had been delayed.

During this waiting period I decided that it was necessary for me to use the toilet. After using the toilet, I went to wash my hands at one of the many washbasins. There on the washbasin face down was a wristwatch which had a black leather strap. I picked it up and it showed the time as being 10 minutes past 9 that evening. I gave the watch to an airport employee for safekeeping.

This dream, at that moment, meant absolutely nothing to me until many months later...

In May 1967 I left England for Canada. After I had spent a period of time in Canada, the Canadian Immigration Authority agreed that my family would be allowed entry to the country. They were due to arrive at Edmonton International Airport on an evening flight.

Not having any transport to get to the airport, a work colleague volunteered to drive me there.

Shortly after arriving at the airport, it was announced that the flight on which my family were travelling had been delayed. Whilst waiting for this flight to arrive I found it necessary for me to use the airport facilities. After using the toilet, I went to wash my hands at one of the washbasins, and there on the washbasin face down, was a wristwatch with a black leather strap, which when I picked it up showed the time as 10 minutes past 9.

The Rat Trap

In The Beginning

THE SCREAM OF pain from the workshop, accompanied by the swearing of a male voice, jolted Eric out of a deep sleep. Initially, a feeling of fear and dread crept over him, for although he didn't consider himself a coward and was quite willing to stand his ground in a confrontation, at just 5 foot 8 inches tall, and of good strength, he knew his limits. As he sat upright, his heart pounding beyond its normal steady beat, he listened intently to the noise coming from his workshop. He closely monitored the clock by his bedside as the minutes ticked by. Gradually the swearing and painful cries dropped to a whimper, being replaced by:

"Please, someone get me out! Don't let me die, I don't deserve this!"

After what seemed an eternity to him, Eric glanced at the bedside clock and realised that only thirty minutes had passed since his rude awakening. It was now 1.30 AM, being a creature of habit who regularly enjoyed a night of uninterrupted sleep, this event would probably have slight repercussions on his well-being in the morning, maybe resulting in bleary eyes and a slight headache.

As he lay back down snuggling under the blankets and felt the warmth of the bed, a smile crossed his face as he said to himself:

"Finally got you, whoever you are!"

It was 8.15 AM when he woke again, a good hour beyond his normal time. As he listened, he realised that the plaintive cries of pain from the workshop had ceased, and had been replaced by the sound of the birds singing and the trees swaying in the breeze.

Now at the age of forty-three, single for the past five years since his long-time partner Brenda had deserted him after eight years together, he thought he had at last found the near-perfect life. He had lived in Lancashire most of his life on the outskirts of Burnley with his parents, two older sisters Margaret and Linda, and his younger brother David. It was a happy childhood; his happiest time was being close to the wild moorland where along with the other local kids he would roam in the wide open spaces.

Leaving school at seventeen he had various jobs, the one he most despised was working on a factory assembly line filling boxes with whatever was required on any given day. He did, however, appreciate that it did at least give him an income. At nineteen he decided that there must be more adventure in life and applied to enlist in the army. He was accepted into the infantry where he served for ten years. In that time he was dispatched to various trouble spots around the world, often finding it very hard to understand why the rulers of some countries could be so ruthless to their own people, seemingly killing and torturing them for no apparent reason.

On leaving the army he worked for various security companies on their armoured vehicles, delivering and collecting mainly cash transactions. It gave him a sense of responsibility, much as he had held in his army career. It was during this employment that he met Brenda Holingsworth who was to be his partner for the next eight years. When they first met it was not so much love at first sight, but rather a process of gradual bonding. She was the same age as Eric, dark-haired and with a good-humoured approach to life. This attitude enabled her to progress in the catering business, beginning as a waitress in a supermarket café and progressing to head of catering for a national company.

Eventually they bought a house together, on the understanding that should the day ever arrive when they could no longer continue to live together, they would simply go their separate ways and divide equally all of their assets.

Unfortunately for Eric that day did arrive. When Brenda did eventually break the news that she had met someone else it left Eric totally distraught. Unable to dissuade her to reverse her decision they sold the house, dividing as previously agreed all of their assets equally.

It left Eric with no choice but to ask his parents if he could move back in with them until such time as he could find a place of his own. There was plenty of room at his parent's house as his sister Margaret and her husband had emigrated to New Zealand, his sister Linda was an airline stewardess and spent most of her time overseas, and his brother David worked overseas for an oil company.

More Pain

Eric's parents welcomed him back home, assuring him that he could stay as long as he wanted until such time he decided to find another place of his own. It was during this time when he was back home that tragedy struck. Eric's father Danny died.

Eric had retired from a local engineering company after fifty years' employment, his final ten years as a workshop supervisor. He and his wife Doris were enjoying a quiet evening in the garden, when a local twenty-nine-year-old troublemaker, Alan Dakin began creating a noise in the street. Eric's father, although much smaller than Dakin, went out and politely asked him to be a little more considerate towards other people and to quieten down. Dakin's response was to use his fists, knocking him down, whereupon he struck his head on the pavement.

Danny died five days later. Dakin was arrested and the CPS took the decision that he should be charged with GBH. When it came to trial Dakin pleaded guilty and was sentenced to four years in jail. This derisory sentence angered Eric's family, for with good behaviour while he was locked away Dakin would probably be released in two years. And their father, who should have been enjoying his retirement, was gone. Doris never recovered from the shock of losing Danny and passed away a year later. Although it was a heart-breaking time for Eric, his sisters and brother, they decided to carry out their parents' wishes which were upon their deaths to sell the family home, and divide the assets equally between their children.

After the sale of his parent's house Eric's only option was to rent a flat in town whilst he continued to search for a place of his own. What he really craved was a house somewhere out of town. He began searching estate agents who specialised in farm or barn conversion properties. Eventually he found an old farmhouse with a few outbuildings about two miles out of town, located four miles off the main road down a single access road. Stonemoor Farm would be his new home.

A New Life

Although Stonemoor Farm had been empty for a little over a year, it still had an electricity supply to the house and one adjacent outbuilding/workshop. With its two bedrooms, tiny kitchen and an open fireplace it was perfect, and the open wildness of its location suited Eric perfectly. In the farmyard was a collection of old tractors and machinery which weeds were gradually beginning to envelop.

The estate agents informed Eric that the owners were a David and Doris Coupland, who had retired from farming over a year previously. Through the estate agents Eric arranged an interview with the Coupland's, who now lived in a bungalow on the outskirts of Burnley. They were in their late sixties, both with greying hair and weather-beaten features no doubt due to the outdoor life of farming. When Eric introduced himself and said that he would be interested in renting the property they were overjoyed that, at last, someone would be caring for the house where they had spent many happy years. They told Eric that he could have the property for a small monthly rent provided that he made an attempt to gradually clean up the area where the machinery now stood. And with regards to all the old tractors and machinery in the farmyard and outbuildings they would make a decision at a later date of what to do about its disposal.

An hour or so later, Eric decided that he had taken up enough of their time and began to excuse himself from their company. As he shook hands with David, David hung onto Eric's hand.

"Haven't you forgotten something?" he asked Eric.

For a brief moment Eric's brain raced, had he said or done something he shouldn't have. David began to smile as he recognised the slight panic which had crossed Eric's face.

"There is one important thing that we do need from you Eric, your surname and address."

Eric, who by now had begun to blush, breathed a huge sigh of relief:

"Eric Crosby, Flat 14 Alexandra Court, Burnley," he answered.

And as for the long term future of the farm, they assured him that at any time he decided he would like to buy the farm it was his. Thanking David and Doris for their hospitality, he excused himself and left, returning to his flat, hopefully for the final time.

Within a few weeks all of the relevant legal paperwork was complete, and Eric moved into Stonemoor Farm. The kitchen table and chairs were still in the house, as were a few basics - washing up liquid, dusters and a vacuum cleaner. As Mrs Coupland explained, even though they had not lived in the house for quite some time they did occasionally visit it just to keep the place tidy.

Within two weeks Eric had the place fixed up to his liking. Having sufficient funds from his share of the sale of his parent's house, he decided to end his employment at the security company and concentrate on gradually cleaning up the overgrown site at the farmyard. This was to prove to be the turning point in his life.

Chopping out all the weeds from around the machinery was a slow, time-consuming task, after which it all had to be dragged clear of the farm. Three weeks later Eric had all the weeds chopped out, with the old tractors and machinery standing silently like statues from ancient times. Disposing of the weeds and rubbish from the farmyard was an easy task once he had dragged them into an adjoining field. With the wind blowing away from the farmhouse all that was required was a few newspapers and a box of matches. A few hours later all that remained was a pile of smouldering ash. After all of the heavy work he had carried out at the farm he decided that he needed a few days' rest, and so he opted for a weekend in a B&B in the Derbyshire Peak District.

It was Monday lunchtime when he returned to Burnley, deciding on the spur of the moment to visit David and Doris Coupland. As he raised his hand to knock on the door of their bungalow it was opened by David Coupland. He took Eric's hand, shaking it warmly.

"I saw you walking up the garden path. So good to see you again Eric, you're certainly looking fit. Doris put the kettle on and make this man a cup of tea."

"Yes dear," came the reply.

He ushered Eric through to the lounge where they chatted briefly until Doris came in with the cups of tea, scones and biscuits. Eric explained that he had just had a few days break in Derbyshire as he needed a rest after all of the work he had done at the farm. His previous employment at the security firm which involved no physical effort had left him out of shape.

Eventually after several cups of tea, scones and biscuits Eric decided it was time for him to return back to the farm. As he began to rise from the armchair David indicated for him to remain seated.

"Eric, we don't want you to think we were both being nosy, but yesterday we decided to have a drive out to the farm and pay you a visit to see how you were settling in. We both felt a little guilty at our suggestion that you could have the farm for a smaller monthly rent if you cleared up the farmyard."

For a brief moment Eric wasn't certain how he should reply as this had caught him totally off guard.

"And when we arrived at the farm we could not believe how you had transformed the place." David continued, "There aren't enough words of gratitude to thank you for all of the hard work you have put into it. So last night, Doris and I had a long chat, and decided that as a thank you for all of your efforts at the farm, you can have all of the tractors and equipment to dispose of as you think fit, including anything in the outbuildings."

"And please Eric, we will understand your possible reluctance to accept this offer, but we have made a decision and this is a far easier approach for both of us rather than us getting involved with auctioneers and suchlike. I spoke to our solicitor this morning and he agreed to prepare the necessary legal papers. So Eric, would this be acceptable to you?" David asked.

Eric sat back in the armchair unable to think of anything to say. He had never been an emotional type of person, but this sudden announcement had left him on the verge of tears.

Eventually, after what seemed an age, he accepted their offer, expressing his profound thanks and gratitude. As he said goodbye there were hugs and tears all round. He drove very slowly back to the farm, still trying to come to terms with what he had been given.

The Auctioneer

He was up early that bright Tuesday morning to survey his achievement of clearing up the farmyard. Gazing across at the tractors and machinery, he still found it hard to believe that David and Doris had been so generous.

He first decided that if he was going to be moving anything of a heavy nature he would require a more robust vehicle, which would

9

come in handy for what appeared to be a large pile of scrap metal underneath a tarpaulin sheet at the rear of one of the outbuildings. Trading in his car he bought a ten-year-old Land Rover together with a heavy duty trailer. His next stop in Burnley that day was a second-hand tool shop where he bought himself a selection of spanners, an electric welding machine and some oxyacetylene cutting equipment.

Having had little free time to himself because of all his work he decided to stop off at a newsagent and buy a newspaper. As he mulled over which newspaper to buy, he spotted a copy of a magazine relating to farm equipment and collectables. Could be interesting, he thought to himself, as he picked up a copy along with his newspaper, paid for them and made his way home.

That evening after supper he sat by the open fire reading the newspaper, when he suddenly realised he had left the farming magazine on the kitchen table. Picking up the magazine he began scanning through its pages. What first caught his attention was the value of old and not so old tractors and machinery being sold at auction. Having been busy for the past few weeks he had never taken account of how many tractors and machinery there were in the farmyard.

As the warmth of the fire slowly took its hold on him, the magazine slipped from his grasp as his eyelids drooped.

The coldness of the air woke him and it took a brief moment for him to gather his thoughts. The fire was now just a few glowing embers and with the clock showing 11.15 PM he headed off to his bed.

After breakfast the following morning he went out into the farmyard to begin making a list of the tractors and machinery. He counted five tractors of various ages, two of which were beginning to show their age but didn't yet look ready for the scrap heap. Some of the machinery was unfamiliar to him but he did recognise a seed drill, baler, and an old combine harvester which looked to be in quite good condition.

On removing the large tarpaulin sheet from what he had previously thought was a pile of scrap metal behind one of the outbuildings, he discovered it was in actual fact a collection of diesel engines, gear boxes, plus an assortment of spare parts, including cylinder heads, valve springs and valves, all of which had been carefully covered in grease to help preserve them against the elements. Whoever it was who collected these did at least have the foresight to stack them clear of the ground onto a twelve-inch-high wooden base. Counting them up there were twenty diesel engines, twenty-five gear boxes and eighteen cylinder heads, some of which looked to be brand new. Why he thought would anyone collect these.

There were three large outbuildings, all of which had double opening doors which were secured by heavy duty locks. Using the keys given to him by David Coupland he unlocked the door to the first building and swung it open. Stepping inside he was greeted by the smell of baled straw, which filled half of the building. The only other item in there was a trailer which had probably been used to move the bales. The second building he opened contained an assortment of feed troughs, fence posts, barbed wire, and other paraphernalia associated with the welfare of farm livestock. The third building was empty, but appeared to have been used like the first one as a store for hay, straw and other farm crops.

Following David Coupland's suggestion he decided to contact an auctioneer to discuss the sale of the farming equipment. Scanning through the pages of the agricultural magazine, one auctioneers name caught his eye, Andrew Fothergill & Sons, Highland House, Burnley. On contacting Mr Fothergill and providing him with a brief description of what was for sale he agreed to visit Eric at the farm the following afternoon.

The sound of a vehicle coming along the road into the farmyard the next afternoon brought Eric out from the outbuilding-workshop, where he had been busy sorting through the various boxes of nuts and bolts which had been left piled on the workbench.

Climbing out of the Land Rover was a tall muscular looking person with a ruddy complexion who Eric guessed to be about sixty years old. From underneath his deerstalker hat protruded tufts of grey hair. At first glance Eric concluded that Andrew Fothergill was a no-nonsense forceful person and he was soon to be proven right. Reaching back inside the Land Rover he retrieved his clipboard, slamming the door shut with such force it made Eric wince.

"Andrew Fothergill, Eric Crosby I presume, pleased to meet you," his voice boomed out, at the same time shaking Eric's hand, his huge hand which dwarfed Eric's almost crushing it.

"Do you know, Eric… don't mind if I call you, Eric? I remember coming to this farm when I was eight years old with my grandfather, when David Coupland farmed it. Quite a surprise when you told me he had retired, still time marches on."

He began to write on his clipboard.

"Now young man, let's go and see what you have got for sale," he said, at the same time marching off across the farmyard.

Eric followed, only catching up with him when he began logging down details of the machinery. So far, Eric had barely had the opportunity to utter a word. After what seemed an age detailing all the farm machinery, they finally reached the tarpaulin which covered the diesel engines and gearboxes.

"And what, might I ask, do we have under here young man?" he asked.

Eric unfastened the ropes which held down the tarpaulin, drawing it back to reveal what lay beneath. Andrew Fothergill's mouth dropped open in disbelief.

"My goodness, my goodness, you lucky man!"

"You mean they are something special?" Eric replied.

"Something special, these are worth a small fortune! Some must be thirty, forty years old. I assume you'll want these included in the sale," he said, writing vigorously on the clipboard.

"Of course you do," he said not giving Eric a chance to reply.

"Right, that seems to be everything in order, Eric," his overpowering voice not giving Eric a chance to say a word.

Handing Eric a copy of what he had listed, together with his company's terms, fee's and conditions, he politely refused a cup of tea. He stopped as he was about to climb into his Land Rover.

"Nearly forgot young man, in a few days you should receive an official sales agreement, if you are happy with the contents just sign and return it. The next upcoming auction is in six weeks' time. Must get on, time is money!"

As the Land Rover sped off down the road in a cloud of dust, Eric couldn't help but smile to himself, at the same time thinking, there goes a man on a mission and nothing will stop him.

The Cheque

Five days later a large brown envelope from Fothergill & Sons arrived via Eric's PO Box in Burnley, which he had established soon after moving into Stonemoor Farm to help protect his privacy. He much preferred driving into Burnley to collect his mail rather than having it delivered. Reading through the contents and finding everything to his satisfaction he signed the agreement and placed it in the prepaid return envelope, then suddenly remembering that he was going into Burnley that same day he decided to deliver it in person.

Two days later a phone call from Fothergill auctioneers informed him that they would be sending a team of men the following morning to Stonemoor Farm to begin the removal of the tractors and machinery.

He was up early the next morning in preparation for the arrival of the removal team. At 8 o'clock the team of men from Fothergill's arrived to begin removing the machinery. This gave Eric the perfect opportunity to continue rearranging the workshop. Later that same evening with all the machinery gone and the workshop just about to his satisfaction he decided it was time for his evening meal and an early bed time.

For the next six weeks he busied himself around the farm, and with building extra cupboards for the workshop.

The date of the auction soon arrived. Wednesday was allocated as the viewing day for potential buyers, so Eric decided it would be a good opportunity to see just how things were laid out. The auction site was located three miles outside of Burnley. Arriving at around 10 o'clock that morning he was surprised by how few people were there. Expecting to find just farm machinery for sale he was amazed by the number of unrelated items such as old bicycles, zinc bathtubs, old rusty spanners and assorted boxes of engine spares.

As he stood looking at a box of engine spares he fell into conversation with an elderly man, who informed Eric that he had been coming to auctions for over twenty years, not to buy anything but just to enjoy the atmosphere. Eric explained that he had never been to an auction before, then referring to the boxes of engine spares and other smaller lots scattered about he asked the elderly man if they ever attracted many buyers. The elderly gentleman told him these items were always a popular buy, as there was a great demand for anything old, and especially engine spares, some of which had ceased production.

"All it takes is a little research," he said.

Eric's curiosity was immediately aroused. He arrived early that Thursday morning at the auction. All of the smaller lots for sale were located away from the main sales area of the large farm machinery, which meant that he would not have the opportunity to see how much his machinery would sell for. Armed with a brochure of the smaller lots for sale, he began making notes of the prices each one sold for. Although it was a time-consuming process which lasted for nearly four hours, he came away highly satisfied with the information he had collected.

The following day he began the arduous task of scanning the internet, researching each of the items which had been sold at the auction, to find out if any were of value on the open market.

He discovered that the elderly gentleman was correct, engine spares always attracted high prices. These were always in demand by restoration enthusiasts. Old spanners were another item much loved by steam engine enthusiasts. Buying a selection of magazines related to the renovation of tractors, motor cycles, and steam engines, he slowly built up his knowledge of what to buy at auction. The more he read the more he felt drawn towards a life of buying auction lots and selling them on.

The next thirty days passed quickly as Eric spent most of his time researching on the computer. Each Friday he would go into Burnley to do his grocery shopping and collect his mail from his PO Box. His mail consisted of the usual pile of sales flyers, a bank statement and a brown envelope which had the stamp mark on the outside from Andrew Fothergill & Sons Auctioneers, Highland House, Burnley. Staring at the name on the envelope he realised that because he had become so engrossed in his research he had forgotten about the auction of his own farm machinery. Deciding to open the envelope back at the farm, he placed it deep down into his inside jacket pocket for safe keeping and continued with the grocery shopping.

Once back at the farm he put away the groceries, made a cup of tea and sat down at the table. He had hung his jacket on the opposite kitchen chair. Looking at the jacket he realised that he still hadn't opened the letter from Fothergill's. Reaching across the table he pulled out the envelope from his inside jacket pocket, sat down and tore it open.

Out dropped a sheet of paper containing an itemised list of what his machinery had sold for, and a cheque to the value of £176, 520.

The Tears

For a moment he sat staring at the cheque in utter disbelief, trying to comprehend the amount of money he now had in his hands. After this initial shock a feeling of self-guilt began to emerge. David and Doris Coupland had been very generous in their offer of gifting Eric the farm machinery, but how could he keep such a large amount of money he thought. Reaching for the telephone he made arrangements to visit them the next day.

At 10 o'clock the following morning he arrived at their bungalow where Doris ushered him into the lounge. David, who had been sitting by the window reading a newspaper, stood up as Eric entered and shook his hand. Sitting down Eric waited until Doris joined them. As Eric tried to clear his throat, at the same time trying to find the words to explain his embarrassment at being presented with such a large amount of money, David and Doris began to smile.

"Eric," David said. "We can guess why you are here, is it about the money from the auction sale?"

Eric looked at them and nodded. He tried to explain that it didn't seem right that he should receive all this money, just for cleaning up the farmyard.

"We were both at Fothergill's auction sale that day," David said. "And although we didn't keep any notes on the amount of money the machinery made, it made us both happy to know that it was going to someone such as yourself, especially as you had the good nature and honesty to come and tell us how much you had received. Some people would have walked away without giving us a second thought."

"We are both well provided for financially, we have no immediate family to pass along our assets too, so the money is yours to spend as you wish."

Tears began to well up in Eric's eyes, which were spotted by Doris who quickly suggested to David that they should both go into the kitchen and make a pot of tea. This gave Eric sufficient time to wipe away a few tears. As they drank their tea they asked him what his future plans were. As Eric outlined his plans, David agreed that it was possible to make a satisfactory business out of it. Before departing Eric shook David's hand and kissed Doris on the cheek, thanking them once again for their generosity, while finding it hard to conceal a tear.

Once out of town he turned onto the road leading back to the farm, pulled the Land Rover over to the side of the road, shut off the engine, broke down and sobbed.

The Break In

The next few months were a learning curve for him. Visiting auction sites around Burnley he was content to bid for just a few small lots, gradually building up his knowledge and confidence, until he knew which the best buys were and what to avoid. He soon discovered that by following the private sales in the free weekly newspaper there were some good bargains to be had, especially someone moving house and having a clear out of their clutter. This kept him busy on days when there weren't any auctions. He used one of the outbuildings for storage, separating everything into different sections relating to their application. In between the days when there was nothing to buy he would spend time in the workshop, cleaning and itemising things for sale. From the outset the most time-consuming aspect was the research required to ascertain the value of different items. However, as his experience grew research began to be a thing of the past, enabling him to spend more time in the workshop.

To continue preserving his privacy he decided to advertise his sales only in certain newspapers and magazines, giving out only his PO Box for any replies, which he collected twice a week from Burnley. The twice weekly visit into Burnley served a dual purpose, as it also gave him the opportunity to deliver customer orders via a courier service in town. Not forgetting the generosity given to him by David and Doris, he would call in to see them once a week, for without their help and the added finance from the machinery sales he would have been looking for employment, as his savings had begun to dwindle.

As the business increased he began to show a substantial profit. Expanding his travel beyond the immediate area of Burnley he slowly built up a list of reliable contacts, which he achieved through his honesty and goodwill. He felt full of happiness that Saturday morning in July as he headed towards the workshop with the intention of tidying up the mess on the work bench which he had created the previous week.

Approaching the workshop he stopped and his heart sank. The one window in the workshop stood wide open. Fearing the worst, he undid the padlocked door and stepped inside. Whoever had broken in had been very selective in what they had taken, as after careful examination of what might have been stolen, the only things that seemed to be missing were Eric's combination spanners, screwdrivers, and a socket set. That was until he looked under the workbench - three old petrol carburettors, which he had lovingly cleaned and restored just waiting to be dispatched to a customer, had been taken.

Trembling with rage he went outside to try and find any signs of vehicle tracks. The only visible tyre tracks he could find were beneath the open window and these were of a narrow type, followed closely by narrower tyre marks about eighteen inches apart. Taking a deep breath, he decided that the first thing he must do was to make the workshop secure. Should he telephone the police and report the offence? Waste of time he thought, what could they do. He replaced the broken glass in the window through which the burglar had reached to unfasten the latch. He then welded together a steel frame, which he bolted onto the brickwork covering the window inside the workshop.

Satisfied that everything was now secure, he drove into Burnley and bought another padlock and hasp for the workshop door as an added security measure. Prior to this burglary he had considered fitting an alarm system, but concluded that living in such an isolated location with no neighbours nearby it would be a waste of money. He was also convinced that anyone who had succeeded in committing one burglary would be back again for a second attempt.

During the drive into Burnley he turned his thoughts back to a few months earlier when he was in one of the farm outbuildings removing a rat from a trap. If only, he thought. By the time he returned from Burnley and fitted the second padlock to the workshop door he had mentally designed the trap. The following day the trap was built and securely fastened onto the floor in the middle of the workshop. On the lid of the box-shaped trap, which measured about eighteen inches' square by two feet deep, he had painted in large letters:

KEEP OUT
DO NOT OPEN
PRIVATE PROPERTY

For the next two months all was quiet at Stonemoor Farm.

A Rat in the Trap

Getting dressed, Eric made his way downstairs and into the kitchen, switched on the kettle for a cup of tea and made his toast. His mind was now in turmoil as he paced around the kitchen eating his breakfast. Whoever it was in the workshop, they had been very quiet for the past few hours. Were they dead? If so, he could be in serious trouble. His hand trembled as he placed the empty tea cup on the table. Slipping on his work boots and tying the laces he made his way the short distance to the workshop. Outside, near the workshop door, stood a bicycle which had a small trailer attached to it by means of a pivot. No wonder he had not heard anything the night of the first burglary, he thought. Both padlocks had been forced from the door using a jemmy bar which lay just inside the doorway.

Stepping in through the doorway and looking towards the trap he found himself staring into the stubbled face of a cold trembling figure that had one arm inside the trap, his other arm somehow twisted beneath his body. His trembling had obviously been caused by spending hours on the cold stone floor. Initially Eric began to feel a pang of sympathy towards him as it brought back memories of the suffering he had seen during his army service. That soon changed however, as he took a closer look at him. It was none other than Alan Dakin, his father's killer. Dakin tried to raise himself with his free arm, at the same time grimacing in pain from the arm still firmly entrapped.

"Get me out of here you bastard," he snarled at Eric. "I will kill you when I get free!"

Eric's sympathy immediately drained away.

"Tell me something," Eric asked. "Didn't your time in prison teach you anything, not even respect for other people? Why do you find it necessary to steal?"

Dakin stared at him. "How in hell's name do you know I had been in jail?" he yelled.

"Oh, Mr Dakin," Eric said mockingly. "I know everything about you, because you are the one who killed my father! And as for you calling me a bastard, you might be a big man with a big mouth, but you seem to forget that you are now under my control, so I suggest that you speak to me with some respect!"

"When you broke into that box and began pulling out the contents it tripped the mechanism releasing the steal jaws inside, similar to a bear trap," said Eric.

"Let me explain a little further about that trap which now holds you. I fitted it with a ratchet system which has locked onto your arm and only I know how to unlock it. So if I decide at any time to walk away and leave you, you would eventually die and rot, which I think would be a very good thing for the rest of mankind. And after your demise the only thing required would be the disposal of your corpse on the moors, perhaps you may be useful after all, as fertiliser."

There was no immediate response from Alan Dakin. Then trying once again to raise himself up, and with his face twisted in pain, he erupted into a rant and rage.

"Your father, your father, yes I killed that doddering old bastard! What use was he to anyone? They said at my trial he had been enjoying his retirement after working all his life. Well ring the bells, I'm glad the bastard is dead, and you will be joining him when I get free!!"

Eric didn't remember picking up the pickaxe handle or beginning to beat Dakin across his body, from which the blood soon began soaking through his clothing. His only recollection was of Alan Dakin's screams of pain.

"Well I must admit, that is the finest piece of punishment I have seen given out in the past twenty years! What do you think, Alec?"

Spinning around Eric was confronted by two heavily built, smartly dressed men in immaculate dark suits, matching ties and smart black shoes. Still breathing deeply from wielding the pickaxe handle, Eric's first thought was that these must be the police. His sheer outrage which had been directed wholly at Alan Dakin had resulted in him not hearing their black van arrive, which he could now see parked outside the open doorway.

The one referred to as Alec stood blocking the doorway.

"Put down the handle," he said to Eric.

The hard look and menacing tone suggested to Eric that it would be a wise thing to obey. The pickaxe handle clattered to the floor.

"Is that our Mr Dakin?" said the first one, who seemed to be in charge.

"Yes," Eric replied

"Release him."

Eric went across to the workbench and reached into a drawer. Taking out a socket wrench he went over to where Alan Dakin was lying and moaning. Fitting the socket wrench onto the trap release mechanism he levered open the jaws. Dakin gave a cry of pain as he rolled free.

"Alec, in to the van with him."

Alec strode over to where Dakin lay, grabbed him by the feet and dragged him screaming across the farmyard. Stopping at the rear door of the van he produced a piece of rag which he stuffed into Alan Dakin's mouth to muffle his cries. Then opening the van door, he heaved him inside slamming the door behind him.

"Now you," said the first man addressing Eric. "You have not seen anything or know anything, do you understand?"

Eric nodded.

"Therefore I bid you goodbye sir," he said as he walked out and climbed into the van.

The van engine roared into life and they were gone. The next edition of the weekly newspaper bore the headline:

LOCAL THUG DISAPPEARS
Police are trying to trace the whereabouts of local man, Mr Alan Dakin in connection with an assault on a suspected drug dealer.

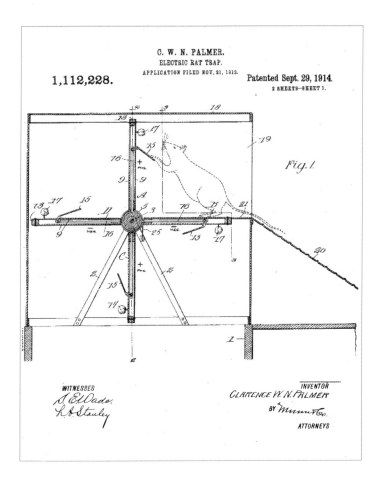

C. W. N. PALMER.
ELECTRIC RAT TRAP.
APPLICATION FILED NOV. 21, 1912.

1,112,228.

Patented Sept. 29, 1914.
2 SHEETS—SHEET 1.

Fig. 1.

WITNESSES

INVENTOR
CLARENCE W. N. PALMER
BY
ATTORNEYS

Old But Happy

Some may find it funny as I wander room to room,
Trying to remember what I was going to do.
Now sit down, pause awhile, have a little think.
That is it, remember, a cup of tea to drink!

A cup of tea to drink, now whereabouts was that?
Last thing I recall I was feeding Joe the cat.
Now was it in the kitchen? Joe is now outside,
I don't think he would take it, he'd prefer to hide.

That is it, the bedroom! Oh joy my brain it shone.
Shuffled to the bedroom, my cup of tea had gone!
Giving up the search, pots to wash upon the sink,
There is my cup of tea, it's good to have a drink.

Now get a piece of paper, shopping list to write.
Was it jam I needed or a pound of tripe?
Cat food I have plenty, pen I begin to lick.
What is that retching sound? Joe the cat's been sick!

Put my coat on, comb my hair, into the mirror grin.
Close my eyes when seeing, the hair upon my chin.
Off down the road, steady limp, now something I have missed.
Searching in my pocket, forgot the shopping list!

Last time I saw my husband was in the potting shed,
Very strange because, thought he was still in bed.
Talking to himself, putting seeds into the pot,
Still it keeps him happy, though he does swear a lot!

Our neighbours house caught fire, her life she thought had gone.
She shouted as they rescued her, "I have clean knickers on!"
What will we have for tea, salad or some stew?
My husband he's not bothered, anything will do.

Crossed the road with care, but stepped into a puddle,
Shake my head and laugh, my brain is in a muddle.
Golden years are great, like floating on a raft.
It's only our good humour that stops us going daft!

The Receptionist

The surgery was quiet the day that I walked in,
Receptionist was dour, couldn't raise a grin.
I said to her I'd been hit with a brick,
Her icy glare in reply nearly made me sick.

Why did I come into this place? I ask.
And meet a woman who'd look better with a mask!
But this is the world we live in, and when we suffer pain,
Mentally it's stressful, experience we gain.

Picking up her pen, she wrote my name on a pad.
Standing there I thought, why is she so mad?
Finally she raised her head, one more icy glare,
Without a word eyes said that I take a chair.

Walked across the room, sat down on a chair,
Contemplated suicide, the silence hard to bear.
Looked down at the floor and my dirty shoes,
Didn't bother to clean them since going on the booze.

Clasped my hands, undid them, drummed fingers on my knees.
Silence overpowering, much colder I will freeze!
Raised my gaze overhead, dare I take the chance,
And lower my eyes after furtively giving her a glance.

This I did, but she was quick, and swiftly did espy,
Caught me out immediately, giving me the evil eye.
Profoundly shocked, my countenance slack,
Was that a knife sticking in my back?

So once more with eyes raised up high,
I took a deep breath, gave out a sigh.
Boredom now was creeping in,
Better not chance giving her a grin.

Suddenly it came clear, why sit around and mope,
Brighten up your thoughts, live a life of hope.
Think of your past happiness, the laughter in your life,
Nights spent in the pub, the wrath of your good wife.

Those were the days of long ago, settled with a kiss,
Hugs and cuddles on a seat, what a life of bliss.
Now she has decided you sit at home and drink,
Makes you follow orders, and just how you think.

But now I am older, these things I accept.
Life is so much easier; I do love being kept!
Though she does nag, her love is deep,
But I love her more when she goes to sleep!

Through all our troubles I still love her lots.
Though she was angry with me for not washing the pots.
And just when I need some peace and rest,
She has to be the damned Receptionist!

Frogwatch

Over the road hippety-hop,
Some frogs make it, others do not.
They are so slow, devoid of dash
Under the wheels, succumb to squash.
I stand at the ready with helping hand,
Giving out aid to this hardy band.
Lifting, carrying, O what a bond,
Giving them life in my little pond.
As daylight ends, my day is complete,
No more rescues out on the street.
Lock up the doors, it's time for tea.
Now I relax, it's my time for me.
Into the bath, what joy this dip.
Donning night clothes, so warm my slip.
My eyes are tired, off to bed I must go,
Climbing the stairs ever so slow.
Bedroom curtains I open wide,
One last look at the World outside.
A look at the road and what do I spot?
An object, a shape, it must be a frog.
Housecoat on, slippers on feet,
Shuffle downstairs, head for the street.
Unlock the door and garden gate.
Hang in there froggie, rescue awaits.
Hurry, hurry, I must be brief,
Bending to the rescue, that frogs a leaf!
Where did this come from? I certainly know not.
Now get off to bed you silly old clot!

Glowing

HAVING ALREADY SHAKEN off the effects of a bitterly cold day which seemed to penetrate his every fibre, Harold gazed into the flames of the fire and felt the comforting warmth on his face. As he pondered his past life, giving the occasional wry smile for his good times, a grimace for the bad, he thought, no one should have to carry out manual work outside, especially at my time of life, 60 years old. After another hard day out in the fields cutting vegetables and being paid just a minimum wage, he hoped he would never see another cabbage again. Still looking on the bright side at least he had a job, and tomorrow he would be cutting sprouts or turnips.

Arriving home at 6.15 PM he decided to leave the car on the driveway, being too tired to open the garage, and anyway he would need it in the morning. Opening the front door of the house, he stepped inside only to be met by the ice-cold air of the kitchen. The central heating had failed to come on again, damn it Harold cursed to himself. This was the third time in two weeks that it had failed.

He decided to light the coal fire in the living room before he began cooking his supper. His wife wouldn't be home from her job at the local hospital until 8 PM, by which time, with the fire stoked up, the house would be nice and warm. He had filled up the coal scuttle before leaving for work that morning but then remembered there were no firelighters. Giving a loud sigh he resigned himself to the fact that it would be necessary to chop some sticks. His already deflated well-being sank even lower on discovering that the only wood available for chopping into sticks was damp.

"Oh what the hell, it will have to do," he muttered under his breath, as he chopped fiercely at the wood.

Gathering up the pieces of damp wood he stomped in through the kitchen, stopping briefly to turn on the gas cooker to warm up his supper. Crouching down by the fireplace he used the remains of an old newspaper on which to place the sticks, then with a trembling hand struck a match under the newspaper which immediately burst into flames. Placing a few small pieces of coal on the sticks, happy in the knowledge that he had at least succeeded in one small task, he gave a contented smile, stood up and with a sigh of relief headed into the kitchen to prepare his supper.

Ten minutes later he removed his supper from the cooker, turned on the radio to hear the local news and sat down for a well-deserved meal. He ate his meal slowly, as he always did, for over the years he had developed a habit of pondering his past fortunes and misfortunes which seemed to take him into a dreamlike world. On occasions, he would miss his mouth with a fork full of food and wipe it down his cheek.

The sudden thought of his attempt to light the living room fire brought his mind back into focus. Putting the last piece of potato hurriedly into his mouth he headed into the living room. His joy turned to anger as he gazed at the few wisps of smoke coming from the fireplace, instead as he expected, glowing coals.

"Right, I will fix you!" he said loudly, striding off into the garage and slamming the kitchen door behind him. Moments later and a little calmer, he went back into the kitchen for a cup of tea.

He must have fallen asleep, as he woke with a sudden start. Looking up at the kitchen clock it was already 7.45 PM.

"I should have a look at that fire just to make sure it's okay," he mumbled to himself.

His wife Elsie would be home soon. Upon opening the living room door, he was shocked and surprised at the glow from the fire. Harold automatically moved his head to the right as a hot particle of burnt wood spat out of the fire narrowly missing his face. The front door by now was almost gone, the heat was so intense that he took two more paces back. Why, he thought, did I put petrol on the fire to give it a boost?

"Still, I'm so glad I had a good quality wooden door fitted as plastic makes such a mess when it melts," he said to himself, whilst giving a comforting shrug of his shoulders.

"What happened?" Elsie asked.

Being so absorbed by the fire Harold hadn't noticed the arrival of his wife Elsie. Harold rolled his eyes up to the heavens at the same time pondering whether he should answer truthfully, or tell her some ludicrous story that aliens had descended that very evening and the heat from their engines had caused the roof to ignite.

"The house caught fire," he replied sarcastically.

A look of sheer frustration and anger, combined with an instant rise in her blood pressure made it impossible for Elsie to give an immediate answer. With clenched fists and through gritted teeth she finally managed to speak:

"I can see the house caught fire, but what caused it?"

"Flames," Harold said, who was still in a state of frustration at his wife's first question about what had happened.

What sort of person, he thought, would, on seeing their home in a total inferno, ask what had happened? One adjective entered his mind. Thick! Before she could give an angry response to Harold's remark the roof of the house fell in throwing up a shower of sparks.

"I'm certainly glad we didn't decorate the upstairs rooms, because that would have been a complete waste of money now this has happened," Harold continued airily. "At least we are insured, I think."

"And where do you think we are going to sleep tonight?" Elsie shouted angrily.

Harold's brow furrowed, his lips slowly moving as though they were trying to communicate with his brain:

"Well, in the garage there is a foldaway bed and as it looks like it is going to be a clear night with no rain we could manage to sleep out under the stars. And with the heat from the smouldering rubble that should be sufficient to keep us warm. But if you are not happy with that my dear there is always the back seat of the car, you know just like our courting days."

Elsie's right hand, which held her handbag and a bag of groceries, swung in a wide arc towards Harold's head. From the corner of his eye, Harold glimpsed the impending blow and ducked down, the intended missile narrowly missing its target. The momentum of Elsie's action continued and swung her off her feet, resulting in her coming to rest on her back with her legs in the air. Harold hurriedly pulled Elsie's skirt back down, at the same time looking around to see if any of the firemen had seen Elsie's underwear.

"Now is not the time to get embarrassed over what I said about spending time on the back seat of the car, after all, apart from getting all hot and sweaty nothing really happened, did it?" Harold said, as he helped her back onto her feet.

"I was looking forward to a cup of tea when I came home from work," said Elsie angrily. "Instead what have you done, you've burnt the house down!"

"Well it was accidental," Harold replied. "I only used a small amount of petrol to boost the damp sticks, and the meat and potato pie you left for me didn't get wasted, because I ate it all before the whole house caught fire. And very tasty it was my dear."

Harold's brief act of wit and sarcasm ended swiftly as Elsie's bag of groceries connected with the side of his head.

It Helps If You're Daft

Do plants make a noise when through the soil they push?
I have often listened, but all I hear is hush.
One day I did decide, as I got ever keen,
I would listen even closer, and lay on the grass so green.
With ear pressed to the ground, motionless I lay,
Oh what bliss, happiness on a summer's day.
Time it seemed so slow, as my vigil I did keep.
Slowly, oh so slowly, I drifted off to sleep.
My neighbour in his garden, basking in the sun,
Glancing over spotted me, assumed that I was gone.
With a burst of energy, he leapt up from his chair
Flinging out his arms, his drink flew through the air.
He raced across the lawn, fearing I was dead,
Tripped over my prone body, landing on my head.
My wife who's pruning roses, let forth a piercing shriek,
Thought that he was a robber, or a total freak.
I remember nothing from that moment on,
Later I was told just what he had done.
Panic then ensued as prostrate I now lay,
What began as pleasant, was now a rotten day.
An ambulance was called, to hospital I was sent,
Grotesque features now acquired, ears bruised and bent.
A&E on alert as they wheeled me in,
Funny looks I got, with weeds stuck on my chin.
Undressing me with care, removing all my clothes.
Upon examination, found soil stuck up my nose,
The doctor asked for tweezers, this he did take out.
"Why," the doctor asked, "is soil pushed up his snout."

Ten days I lay in a coma, before I finally woke
To find a nurse tending me, as my brow she stroked.
"What are you doing?" I did ask, as she gave a gentle smile.
"Why washing you and caring for a little while."
Her beauty overwhelmed me, and then it came to pass,
I told her she'd go far, as she had a friendly aspect!
With these words her cheeks did blush, then she held my hand,
My mind it was in turmoil, wasn't life just grand.
Then the magic it was gone when my wife strode in.
"Come on you, time to go, drop that silly grin!"
My happiness was brief as she marched me out the door.
Never, will I ever, lay down on the floor!

Time

Why does time pass quickly, when one is getting old?
It's in the mind, now that it's gone, something to behold.
We can look back on yonder days, be they good or bad.
When I was young some were tough, as a little lad.
I still can see quite clearly through those eager eyes,
Recalling distant memories with no effort or surprise.
I can recall some happy times, with the time and place,
And of those around us, together with a face.
But past life is different than the reading of a book,
Memory selects and holds no matter how we look.
Why does our brain select and hold such memories
Like a photograph before us, it lingers never dies.
So singular they sit, unable to deviate
No matter how we try they will still await.

Click

The Old Lady

IT WAS A typical raucous Saturday night in July in the Crown and Anchor pub, located on the outer fringes of Manchester. The landlord Jack 'Doggy' Russell, as the locals had nicknamed him, briefly wiped the sweat from his brow as he counted out the change from the till before handing it over to Arthur, one of the few regular drinkers left over from when the pub was the place to have a quiet drink and conversation. Arthur's main reason for his regular attendance at the pub, he told Jack, was the quality of the beer, and certainly not the present clientele. No sooner had he handed Arthur his change, another order for drinks was requested.

As he pulled the next pint of lager he glanced up at the clock on the wall of the bar which showed 10.30 PM. Another thirty minutes and he would be calling time, with a strict rule that no drinks would be served after 11 PM. There would, of course, be the usual moans and groans when he refused to serve anyone after that time, but as he told them, rules were rules and he wasn't prepared to change them. His only help behind the bar at weekends was Margaret, a middle-aged local lady who had spent most of her working life as a barmaid. Margaret had been employed since the sudden death of his wife Molly six years ago. Margaret had a magic way with even the most troublesome, loud-mouthed customers, never taking offence at any crude or rude remarks which were thrown her way, replying only with a pleasant smile.

Jack was now in his early sixties, and having spent nearly all his life in the pub trade had seen many changes over the years. Gone were the days when customers were quite content to share a story or a joke, instead now many of his customers seemed to find it necessary to shout. A far cry from when he first became the landlord of the Crown and Anchor, just over 8 years earlier, when the majority of his customers were middle-aged folk, content to talk quietly and listen to the old-fashioned music which Jack kept at a low volume. Although his profit margins were fairly modest they were sufficient for him to enjoy a comfortable lifestyle.

That tranquillity, along with his middle-aged regulars, disappeared soon after the brewery decreed that a change was needed to bring the pub into the modern age and encourage a more youthful clientele. It took only three weeks of closure for the Crown and Anchor to be modernised. What were formerly two rooms, the bar and the snug, was now one room, the dividing wall having been demolished. The only thing Jack did appreciate was the fresh decoration of the place, along with the new carpets, which had begun to look a little threadbare. The sedate music was replaced by the so-called 'modern rubbish' as Jack called it, which forever gave out a constant thump, which in turn had attracted a growing band of loud, foul-mouthed louts, some of whom, he soon found out, were local thugs who you should never cross.

Even though he kept the music at a low volume the shouting never decreased, especially from a group of six young men who stood at one end of the end of the bar. Every Friday and Saturday night the same group of six would occupy the same spot, and if anyone tried to stand in their way a few hard stares from them soon got their message across. Move or else. The one with the loudest voice and obviously the leader of the pack, was a tall,powerfully built individual called Tommy Anderson.

"Hey Doggy," Tommy shouted. "Another pint of your lousy lager if you have the time, please."

"No problem, sir," Jack replied, reaching for a clean glass.

This response was met with a collective roar of laughter from Tommy's mates, who seemingly wallowed in their own misguided popularity. Having served Tommy his pint of lager there was a brief respite in orders, time which Jack always liked to use to reminisce, especially over the sad loss of his beloved wife Molly. So absorbed was he in his thoughts that he didn't notice Margaret standing up close to him. A petite dark-haired lady with a strong self-determination, she smiled at him as he suddenly broke out of his thoughts.

"A penny for them Jack, or are they personal?" she asked.

"Oh, just thinking back over the years - the good, the bad, and the indifferent. But the really stupid part of all this thinking is, that for all the regrets which we have, we cannot change a thing."

Margaret nodded in agreement: "True, so true," she replied.

"Yes dear, what can I get you? Two pints of bitter and a gin and tonic. Thank you," said Margaret, bringing her conversation with Jack quickly to an end.

For the next ten minutes it was a flurry of activity serving drinks as everyone seemed intent on getting one last drink before the bar closed. As Jack poured another pint of beer, he couldn't help but notice an old lady enter the room from the door which opened out onto the street. She slowly pushed her way through the crowded room in the direction of bar where Jack was serving drinks, before finally passing the area which was occupied by Tommy and his mates.

"Well what have we here? Good evening grandma. Don't tell me, you are on the lookout for a bit of late night fun?!" Tommy shouted, which was followed by the usual roar of approval from his mates.

The old lady, who was dwarfed by the size of Tommy, just turned and through her spectacles glared at him.

"Have you no respect for anyone young man!" she said in a firm voice. For a brief moment Tommy said nothing, as if unable to absorb the fact that anyone would actually confront him regarding his attitude.

"Oh, come on grandma, give me a kiss! I will show you a good time!" Tommy responded.

The old lady who was dressed in a grey coat and carried a large black handbag ignored Tommy and instead turned to Jack.

"I am sorry to bother you, but can I have the use of your toilet, please?" she said.

"You certainly can my dear," Jack replied. "You will find the ladies toilet over there," he said, as he pointed her towards the far wall.

She gave him a warm smile, then turned and made her way through the crowded room towards the toilet. Minutes later and as Jack called for last orders, the door of the ladies toilet opened and the old lady emerged, and began to make her way through the crowd towards the door which led back onto the street. As she approached Tommy, who had observed her coming, he tried to block her path by pretending not to notice her as she squeezed past him whilst he related the end of a joke to his mates.

"Anyway this woman's ca-," Tommy's voice began to fade as his eyes rolled upwards, his face taking on a look of absolute agony.

"Anyw-, any-."

Once again he gasped and strained to complete his joke but to no avail, his knees slowly buckled as he sank to the floor, the remains of his beer spilling down his shirt. By this time Jack and Margaret were inundated with last orders and didn't notice Tommy slowly collapsing into a heap on the floor.

"Hey Doggy," shouted one of Tommy's mates in a sarcastic tone. "Looks like Tommy has finally suffered the effects of your rotten ale!"

Jack peered over the bar and seeing Tommy sprawled out on the floor immediately ran around to where Tommy lay. Just a quick look at Tommy told him this could be an emergency.

"Margaret, can you call for an ambulance?" he shouted.

"Ladies and gentleman, please no more orders. We have someone who requires immediate medical attention, so I ask you please to finish your drinks and make room for the emergency services, thank you."

In the commotion no one observed the closure of the door out onto the street, and the disappearance of the old lady.

The Death of Tommy Anderson

The ambulance arrived within five minutes by which time all of Tommy's so called mates, apart from one Eddy Hargreaves, had finished their drinks and disappeared. As the ambulance crew attended to Tommy, one of them looked up at Jack and shrugged his shoulders as if to indicate that the situation was not good. Two minutes later with sirens wailing the ambulance carried Tommy off to the local hospital. Jack looked around at the now empty silent pub. Although he had never been a great fan of Tommy and his friends, he never wished ill will on anyone. The silence was finally broken by Margaret.

"Have you any idea what might have happened to him?" she asked.

Jack shook his head.

"I don't understand it," he replied.

"Eddy Hargreaves told me that Tommy was telling one of his smutty jokes, then he just slowly sank down. Perhaps it was a heart attack."

"Well anyway Margaret, that is life as they say. We just have to keep soldiering on," said Jack as he began tidying away the mostly empty glasses.

It was after midnight when he and Margaret had finally cleaned and stored all of the glasses. He wished her goodnight and locked the doors, before heading off to bed. She would be back at 9.30 AM on Sunday morning to vacuum and clean for the start of another busy day.

Jack was woken by the sound of the vacuum cleaner that Sunday morning. Rubbing his eyes, he looked at the bedside clock which showed 10 AM, then cursed himself for not being up and about at his usual time of 8 AM. However, due to the previous night's disruption he had tossed and turned trying to come to terms with what had caused Tommy's possible demise. After a quick cup of tea, he made his way into the bar area where Margaret had completed the vacuuming and was now busy polishing the table tops.

"Good morning Jack," she greeted him with her usual pleasant smile. "It's certainly a good thing that you gave me a key to let myself in otherwise I would have been outside banging on the door."

Her voice then faded into a sympathetic tone as she observed the worried look on his face.

"Oh, I am sorry Jack. I hope you didn't think I was being sarcastic. You must have had an awful night thinking about what happened."

Jack, still with a doleful outlook, managed a half-smile and nodded in acknowledgement of her apology.

"Oh, by the way Jack," she continued. "They said on the local radio this morning that Tommy had died, apparently he was pronounced dead on arrival at the hospital."

Jack once again nodded, gave her another half-smile and began checking the cash float in the till.

By 12 noon his spirits had lifted as he greeted the first customers. These consisted mainly of Sunday lunchtime drinkers, who enjoyed a few pints of beer before heading off home for their Sunday dinner. News about Tommy's death had spread throughout the local community, and despite the majority of people expressing their condolences, the jokes and innuendoes soon began to circulate in relation to the beer which Jack sold. Jack just shrugged it off. Only one of Tommy's mates came in that morning, Eddy Hargreaves. He was in his mid-twenties, a quiet type, a bit of a loner. Jack had long ago formed the opinion that Eddy hung around with Tommy's mates because he found it difficult to communicate with anyone outside their little group. In between serving drinks Jack tried to strike up a conversation with Eddy who stood at the end of the bar, where the previous night Tommy had taken his final drink.

"How are you feeling, Eddy? Terrible thing what happened last night, to lose one of your friends so fast."

Eddy took a sip from his drink, then taking a deep breath replied: "I don't understand it, Jack. Here we were, not really bothering anyone, well apart from Tommy who, you know, could be a bit of a pain, then suddenly Tommy collapses and that's it, he's gone."

The remainder of Sunday at the Crown and Anchor passed off quietly, and as Jack bid Margaret goodnight and locked the pub door, he gave a silent prayer in the hope that he would never have another weekend like that again.

The Autopsy

It was 9.30 AM on Monday morning and Detective Inspector Christopher Knowles picked up his office telephone before it had completed its second ring. At fifty-two years old he had been in the Lancashire police force all of his working life. A dedicated no-nonsense officer, he had begun as a regular PC on the beat before transferring to the detective division seventeen years ago.

"Knowles here."

"And how are you this bright and cheerful morning Mr Know-all?" rang out the reply. "Just hope you haven't got your knickers in a twist."

Although 'Chris' or 'Inspector' was his preference, he knew that many in the division referred to him as Mr Know-all because of his

43

knowledge and ability in tracking down criminals. But only a few acquaintances ever directly addressed him by that name. He immediately recognised the caller's voice

"I might have expected a sarcastic call from Brian the Butcher at the slice and dice factory. What is it now, three weeks since you had any grizzly stories to relay? It must be something important for you to be calling this early, you miserable old sod!" he laughed as he spoke.

He had known Brian Booth the Coroner since joining the police force, and was constantly reminded of the time he had fainted when attending his first autopsy.

"What can I do for you Brian, is there a problem?"

"There certainly is, a very strange one. I could say with some certainty that it looks like a murder."

"Where and when did this happen, Brian?"

"In the Crown and Anchor pub on Dartford Street on Saturday night."

"I heard on the radio about someone collapsing and dying in a pub, but apart from that I don't know any more details," Chris replied.

"Anyway Chris, is there any possibility you can get down here to the autopsy department this morning?"

"No problem, Brian. I should be down there in the next hour or so."

Hanging up the phone he busied himself around the office catching up on some urgent outstanding paperwork. He decided to take Detective Constable David Evans with him to the autopsy department. DC Evans had been in the police force for about eighteen months. He was in his early twenties, with a very keen attitude towards learning.

"Where are we off to sir?" he asked as they climbed into Chris's car.

"We, DC Evans, are off to the mortuary," he replied, smiling to himself.

He smiled because he knew that many young constables did not care very much for a visit to the mortuary, as he himself had had first-hand experience.

Thirty minutes later they arrived at the mortuary. Having signed the visitors book they both made their way through the building to Brian Booth's office. A tall, balding, well built person with a hearty laugh, whose looks would make anyone think he was a butcher by trade, shook Chris's hand as they entered his office.

"Good to see you again, Chris. Hope the family is well. And this young man is?" he asked, indicating DC Evans.

Chris introduced him to DC Evans, who by now seemed a little more relaxed. Chris and DC Evans donned their protective gowns, gloves and face masks before following Brian into the pathology department. There was just one body, on a table in the middle of the room, covered by a white sheet. Drawing back the sheet, Brian exposed the naked body of Tommy. DC Evans's face began to slowly lose its colour upon seeing the body. Chris couldn't help but notice this and immediately tried to calm the situation.

"Now come on DC Evans, please don't let the side down. It is just a body, someone who has suffered an unfortunate end to his life. Just take a deep breath and you will be fine."

DC Evans followed his advice.

"Now," Brian said. "When I first looked at the body, apart from a little blood around the mouth there didn't seem to be any other injuries, until we turned him over and examined his sides."

Brian called over two of the pathology technicians, and asked them to turn the body over onto its face.

"Now just take a look here," he said, pointing his finger to the left rear side of the body, about halfway down the ribcage.

There was a bruise about three quarters of an inch in diameter, and as they looked closer, there in the middle of the bruise was the glint of a shiny object.

"What the hell is that?" asked Chris.

"That is just what I asked myself," replied Brian. "So then I did an X-ray and got the answer, follow me."

He led them over to the X-ray scanner, clicked on the light and pointed his finger at the dark object which showed up on the X-ray.

"Now that is a beauty, isn't it? Whoever stuck that into him must have been a pretty powerful person. And if you look closer, they certainly didn't intend for it to be easily removed, because that object has got barbs like you will find on fish hooks all the way down its length. I would say that is a piece of steel, approximately a quarter of inch in diameter, about four or five inches long. That poor soul would not have known what hit him!"

Chris and DC Evans moved in closer to take a look at the X-ray.

"What sort of devious character would do such a thing?" asked Chris as they studied the X-ray. "But then again, in today's world, nothing surprises me anymore."

"I will next set about removing the offending weapon," said Brian. "I will of course keep it in a safe place and forward it on to you ASAP, along with my report and any clues which I may come across. It is also my opinion, just looking at the angle of entry of the weapon, that whoever did this must have been a fairly small person."

"Right, okay Brian, thanks for everything. We will go to the hospital A&E and see what their report says about his admission on Saturday night."

At the hospital A&E they spoke to the duty nursing sister for Saturday night, Sister Dawn Adams. She confirmed that at approximately 23.09 PM the previous Saturday, a Mr Thomas Anderson, age 29, of 92 Briar Avenue, Manchester had been admitted as DOA. And as there were no physical signs of injury his death was recorded as unexplained, until there was a full coroner's report. Taking a copy of the report, Chris thanked her and departed back to his office to begin the task of tracking down those responsible for the death of Thomas Anderson.

Back at his office his first enquiry was into Thomas Anderson's background, and if he had any criminal connections or convictions. Apart from a few minor convictions and police cautions there was nothing of a serious nature to associate him with any big time criminals, and so Chris, along with DC Evans, decided to begin their enquiries where the trail began, at the Crown and Anchor pub. Chris made a phone call to the Crown and Anchor pub and agreed a time with the landlord Jack Russell to interview him that afternoon at 3 PM.

The Enquiry Begins

Arriving at the agreed time, Jack showed them through into his living quarters where he proceeded to give them a report into what happened at the bar the previous Saturday night.

After taking down a brief written statement, Chris asked Jack to show him the exact spot where Tommy had been standing and the location of everyone else who had been in the same vicinity as him. Moving into the bar area Jack began by detailing just where Tommy had been standing with his mates. Then as the questions began to get into a more serious mode, Jack started to get a little uneasy.

"Inspector, excuse me for asking, but these questions seem to be having implications that I do not like. Is there something that you are not telling me? And if anyone doubts my word there is always my barmaid Margaret to confirm my statement as true, you can always speak to her."

"Oh I certainly intend to speak to her, Mr Russell," Chris replied.

"Now, you were saying that Tommy was standing just there," Chris said.

Jack nodded his head.

"David," said Chris addressing DC Evans. "Now you take the position of where Tommy, Mr Anderson, was standing. Now, Jack, I do understand this can seem time-consuming, but the more details I have the easier it will be for me to move forward in understanding how and why Tommy died."

DC Evans was now standing where Jack had indicated.

"And these mates of Tommy's, you say they were stood close to him."

"Yes."

"And how many were there, can you remember?"

"Perhaps five or six, it was difficult to tell as everyone was moving about, getting served with their drinks, as you must understand inspector Saturday night is a very busy night for us."

"Yes of course, Jack."

"And these mates of Tommy's who were with him on Saturday night, do you know their names?"

"Only one, an Eddy Hargreaves who lives on Shaw Street just around the corner from the pub, the rest of them they tended to address each other with ridiculous slang names such as Shug, Beefy etc. If you speak to Eddy I am sure he can help you find their names."

"Have you got all those details?" Chris asked DC Evans, who had been busy writing in his notebook.

Without raising his head, DC Evans nodded in reply.

"Now, Jack, the stage is yours, tell me again, as close as you can, what you remember of Saturday night at just about closing time."

Jack once again went into detail, with DC Evans taking notes of everything that he said.

"And just as I was about to call last orders… Oh, I remember this little old lady as she returned from the ladies toilet had great difficulty pushing her way past Tommy and his mates. Rude lot they could be, no manners at all, in fact-"

"Wait a minute, Jack," Chris interrupted. "What little old lady? You never mentioned this earlier in our conversation, why have you suddenly remembered her?"

Jack took a deep breath as the questioning by now was beginning to annoy him, as if he had something to hide in relation to the enquiry. Jack then described how Tommy had tried to intimidate the old lady when she first walked past him, and the old lady's response to him.

"So you would say that this old lady was a no-nonsense type then, Jack."

Jack nodded in agreement.

"And how old would you say she looked?" Chris asked.

"I would guess about mid to late sixties," Jack replied.

"And can you remember if there was anything different about her, any special features?"

"Well," said Jack. "She just didn't fit in somehow with the usual crowd. Firstly, her dress sense, she wore an old grey coat which was clean enough, no hat, grey hair, but what was noticeable was that she carried a large black handbag."

"And you say that as she squeezed past Mr Anderson that is when he collapsed?"

"Yes," replied Jack. "Oh and one more thing about her, she wore glasses."

"And as she squeezed past Mr Anderson, you didn't hear any unusual noise or see any odd movement amongst the people stood close to him?" asked Chris.

Jack shook his head.

"Have you got all of these details written down, DC Evans?" asked Chris.

"Yes Sir."

"Well I think that is all the details I need for the moment. I will arrange as soon as possible, possibly today Jack, for a police sketch artist to visit you and for you to describe in detail all that you can remember about this old lady, can you do that for me?" asked Chris.

"Yes, of course I can, but can I ask why you want all of these details? Is there something about this matter of a serious nature?"

"Jack, all I can say at this moment is that we have an ongoing investigation, and I ask that you to keep our discussion today just between ourselves. Can you do that for me?"

For the next hour Chris and DC Evans noted down from Jack, all of the possible witnesses who were in the pub that Saturday night. Eventually Chris concluded that he had gathered sufficient evidence from the crime scene, thanked Jack for his patience and departed back to the police station to begin unravelling the mystery as to why anyone would want to kill Tommy Anderson.

The Cat Connection

The following day Chris received the sketch of the old lady of which copies were circulated throughout the police force in the hope that someone might recognise her. Also later that day he received a call from the coroner Brian Booth, who informed him that he had extracted the piece of steel rod from Tommy Anderson's body, and would he like to see it. Together with DC Evans they were down at the mortuary within the next half hour. There in the stainless steel tray which Brian Booth presented to them was a steel rod of about a quarter inch in diameter, between four and five inches long with a sharp point at one end. Along its length there were in the region of twenty to thirty raised barbs. As Brian explained, it appeared to him that the rod had been held in a vice and a hammer and chisel used to cut angles into it to create the barbs. Having photographed the steel rod, they sealed it in an evidence bag and delivered it to the forensic laboratory for further examination.

Their next task would involve an interview with Tommy's parents to try and gain more insight into Tommie's background. And as Chris explained to DC Evans as he rang the doorbell at 92 Briar Avenue, this was one part of his job he had always dreaded, ever since his early days in the force. Having to ask questions from someone about a loved one who had recently died chilled him to the bone.

A tall well-built gentleman who looked to be in his mid-fifties opened the door, who Chris assumed was Tommy's father, Alan Anderson. Chris introduced himself and DC Evans, and after briefly explaining the reason for their visit they were invited inside. Tommy's father ushered them through into the living room and introduced them to his wife, Tommy's mother Anne, a dark-haired petit woman, who began sobbing as Tommy's father explained to her the reason for Chris and DC Evans's visit. Within less than a minute she excused herself and with tears still running down her face she left the room.

Chris swallowed hard, took a deep breath, and trying not to show any personal emotion began the interview with Tommy's father. He began by asking where Tommy had been employed, before asking anything about his background. His father explained that Tommy had been a gardener with the council since leaving school, and three months prior to his death he had just been promoted to assistant head gardener.

"He was very proud of his gardening skills," continued his father. "He could make anything grow."

However, his brow furrowed at one stage when he began relating the slightly darker side of his son's life.

"He got a girl pregnant when he was fifteen, she was the same age, caused a lot of upset I can assure you, especially for my wife. Anyway shortly after the child was born, a little girl, the family moved away. Where too, I have no idea. They didn't even have the decency to tell us what they had named the child."

Then looking directly at Chris he asked: "I assume that before coming here you have already looked into my son's record on the police computer?"

"Yes," Chris replied. "And apart from some minor indiscretions there was nothing of a serious nature on his record."

"Well as his father, quite naturally, I would defend him most of the time, but because of his size he turned out to be a bully towards anyone smaller than himself, and I could not tolerate that at all. And when I found out about his bullying many years ago, I gave him a warning that it had to stop, otherwise he would have me to reckon with, and after that it seemed to stop."

"But my son had a weakness inspector, and not many people knew it. If he bullied anyone and they had the courage to stand their ground and fight back, he would be a complete coward. But for all his faults I still cannot understand why anyone should find it necessary to kill him."

Eventually Chris decided that he had collected enough information regarding Tommy's background, thanked his father for his patience and made his excuses to leave, but not before showing him a sketch of the old lady, at which he shook his head. As he and DC Evans stepped out of the house and down the garden path Tommy's father called them back.

"Inspector Knowles there is one thing that I did forget to mention about Tommy, it may be nothing at all but Tommy had a bitter hatred of cats."

"Cats," Chris replied. "Why cats?"

"Well it was all about his gardening, cats would sometimes scratch about in the soil, make a mess as they do, and he hated it. He took it as personal insult."

Taking out his notebook once again DC Evans made further notes. Thanking Tommy's father, they set off back to police headquarters to collate their findings into the death of Tommy Anderson.

Another One

The following day Chris and DC Evans began the laborious task of tracking down and interviewing potential witnesses to the crime. But the one puzzle which kept nagging away at Chris however, was what sort of device had been used to fire the steel bolt which killed Tommy Anderson. Their interview with Eddy Hargreaves didn't reveal any more clues into the case. He did however, provide them with the names and addresses of Tommy's other friends who were there on the night in question.

After two weeks of interviews not a single piece of evidence had surfaced, and no one recognised the old lady from the artist's sketch. A few days after Chris had reported his findings on the case to his seniors in the force, they decided to publicise the fact that they were treating the death of Tommy Anderson as a possible murder case, without any mention of what killed him. A decision was also taken not to publicise the sketch of the old lady.

DC Evans was out that Thursday morning assisting a uniformed officer with an attempted robbery at a corner shop when the telephone in Chris's office rang. Instantly he had the feeling that this call meant trouble. He had been looking forward to a quiet relaxing weekend with his wife Diane. The weather forecast was perfect. He had bought steaks and chicken, giving him the chance to indulge in one of his favourite pastimes, cooking on his barbeque. He slowly picked up the telephone receiver.

"Inspector Knowles speaking."

"Well I would hope that it is Inspector Knowles speaking, especially when I rang your number. How are things in the 'solve a crime' department these days? You sound like you need a dose of happiness!"

"And what can I do for you Brian the Butcher from the slice and dice? You sound like you have won the lottery!" Chris replied.

"Well, I hate to be the bearer of bad tidings but I have just spoken to your chief inspector and it looks like you have been chosen for a special operation."

Chris's heart sank as he listened.

"And what special operation would that be?" Chris asked.

"We have got another one," Brian replied.

"Another one what?"

"Why none other than a piece of steel in the ribs old boy, same size, complete with barbs, and buried very deep inside some unfortunate person, this time a lady."

Chris sat stunned, unable to speak for a few seconds.

"Where and when did this happen Brian?"

"Last night at a school reunion for an older generation of pupils going back over the last fifty years apparently, so I am reliably informed. The school in question is St Hughes Comprehensive on Park Street."

Inwardly Chris's heart sank. There was now the strong possibility that he would be delegated to work over the weekend on this latest suspicious death, and goodbye to his barbecue. Telling Diane his wife was to be his next hurdle.

"Have you begun the autopsy, Brian?"

"Yes, it's all complete. My report is being typed up as we speak. Can I expect you down here later today?"

"Yes, but first it will be necessary for me to have a meeting with my boss, Chief Inspector Norris."

Thanking Brian for the phone call, Chris hung up the phone and busied himself checking his diary details before ringing Inspector Norris who immediately agreed to a meeting with him in his office.

"Come in, Chris," a voice called out as Chris knocked on Inspector Norris's office door.

Chris entered and Inspector Norris (Colin) who was standing looking out of his office window, turned and invited Chris to take a seat. Colin was a short stocky person in his late-fifties with grey thinning hair, who had begun his career as a PC on the beat, gradually rising through the ranks until he reached his present position in the force. He sat down at his desk facing Chris.

"Chris, no doubt you will have had a phone call from the coroner Brian Booth about this latest death, seemingly caused by a steel projectile of some sort. This time the victim was some poor lady. I have been looking through the case file on the first killing of this nature, and it appears that you and your colleague, a DC Evans, pretty well hit a brick wall in your investigations."

"Well sir…"

Before Chris could continue Inspector Norris held up his hand as a sign of silence.

"Let me continue, Chris. I must admit after reading the details collated by yourself and DC Evans that you did an excellent job, and no doubt you will both press on until someone is brought to justice. Now it seems probable that the same killer or killers have struck again and no doubt senior figures in the force will not be very happy. But as you and everyone in the lower ranks know, we cannot simply wave a magic wand and solve a crime even if those upstairs think we can."

"Being mostly university educated and promoted on their qualifications they would not know the first thing on how to begin an enquiry. Please do not quote me on that! Anyway, I suppose Brian Booth mentioned to you that I had decided that you would be the best man to investigate this latest killing, and take DC Evans with you. I think that young man will go far."

"And one other thing I should mention Chris, if you find that you require extra personnel on this case don't hesitate to give me a call."

Thanking Inspector Norris, he went back to his office from where he phoned DC Evans, asking him to meet him at the mortuary. At the mortuary office Brian Booth showed Chris the piece of steel he had extracted from the latest victim, a widow, Mrs Sarah Middleton. Its dimensions appeared to be nearly identical to the one taken from the body of Tommy Anderson. DC Evans arrived as they were discussing the steel bolt. Handing him the steel bolt Chris asked him:

"DC Evan's, I wish to ask you a question. But before I do I have a confession to make, but please do not tell anyone outside this room what it is. My question is, do you have any theories or ideas as to how someone can inject or stab that piece of steel into someone without apparently making a sound, because I have laid awake at night trying to figure it out, and it is driving me mad? Here I am a senior officer, and I haven't got a clue."

DC Evans sat silently looking at the steel bolt for a few seconds before giving his answer.

"No sorry sir, but I will certainly give it some thought."

Thanking Brian Booth, they then went to the hospital A&E department to collect the report on the admittance of Mrs Sarah Middleton. They spent the next few minutes in Chris's car pondering over the A&E report which was very brief. The report read that at approximately 10.05 PM a Mrs S Middleton of 21 Calver Street was attending a school reunion in the assembly room at St Hughes Comprehensive, Park Street, Manchester when she suddenly collapsed. An ambulance was dispatched which took her to the hospital A&E, but she was pronounced dead on arrival. The only external injuries noted were a round bruise on her rear left ribcage and in the centre of the same bruise was what appeared to be a metal object. The report concluded - awaiting coroner's findings.

"Well DC Evans," said Chris as they drove off from the hospital. "I think you will agree that our first port of call is St Hughes Comprehensive where this dastardly deed took place.

"Yes sir."

A uniformed officer was on duty at the entrance to St Hughes Comprehensive School assembly room when Chris and DC Evans arrived. After showing their warrant cards they then made their way into the assembly room where scene of crime officers were still in attendance, led by Inspector Edward (Ted) Morris.

"Have you picked up any clues, Ted?" Chris asked.

"Not a thing, Chris. We've photographed the complete area where the crime occurred and found nothing, whoever is responsible for the crime is a very clever person or persons. We have contacted the person responsible for organising this reunion, a Miss Agnes Forbes, her address and phone number are on this list, and she said you can contact her at any time."

"I have already spoken to her and she is absolutely distraught over this," said Ted. "Agnes Forbes was standing in the same group of people as Mrs Middleton when she collapsed."

Handing Chris a folder containing his report, he left to continue his work. Chris took a deep breath as he and DC Evans climbed into his car and drove off to conduct another lump-in-the-throat interview. Agnes Forbes lived in a detached bungalow at 36 Union Street. It was a quiet residential area as residents were mostly retired or semi-retired. Chris had phoned her before setting off, and she must have been looking out for their arrival, because the door to the bungalow opened before they had even got out of the car.

"Please come in Inspector, Constable."

Her hands trembled as she showed them through into the lounge.

"Please take a seat. Would you both like a drink, tea or coffee, perhaps a piece of cake or biscuits?"

They both agreed that tea would be acceptable, and she hurried away to fill the kettle. Within a few minutes she returned with the tea. Her hands were still trembling as she sat down opposite them, a small stocky built lady who looked to be in her mid-to-late sixties.

"A terrible business last night at the school," she began. "I was the head teacher there for over twenty years and-."

Chris interrupted her with a polite cough.

"Oh I am so sorry inspector, here I go again. I do so ramble on, but last night… Sarah Middleton had been a dear friend for many many years, and then some terrible thing happens to her."

"Miss Forbes."

"Please inspector not Miss Forbes, you can call me by my first name, Agnes."

"Now I understand Agnes, that you were the person who organised the reunion for the former pupils and teachers from the school, which took place in the school assembly room last night. Have you, by any chance, a list of those people who attended this event?"

"Certainly," she replied, reaching out onto a side table and handing Chris a paper folder. "I have always believed in keeping accurate records. Including myself there was a total of thirty nine people in attendance at the reunion."

Her hands had now stopped trembling, her composure more reassured. Chris briefly looked through the folder at the list of people who had attended the reunion and everyone listed seemed to have been accurately recorded, including their addresses. Chris finally looked up at Agnes.

"According to your, and I must say, very detailed notes, you must have spent a long time tracking down all of these people. When did you begin this task?"

"I began at least nine months ago. It was a task I had considered doing over the last few years. Having never married and with no immediate family I thought it would be a wonderful thing to meet old school friends one last time before I got too old, and then last night turned out to be a complete disaster. So sorry inspector," she said as she dabbed away more tears.

"I understand, Agnes. Now if it's not too painful for you, can you describe as near as possible the events leading up to the moment when sadly Mrs Middleton collapsed in the assembly room?"

Agnes took a deep breath and began relating the events of the previous night. She said that everyone had arrived at the assembly room by eight o'clock, except for two of the three men who had accepted the invitation. The only man to attend was a Mr Michael Andrews.

"Myself and four other ladies had earlier in the day prepared sandwiches, tea and cakes. Guests were invited to bring bottles of alcoholic drinks if they desired. A few did and freely shared them around with others, but no one over-indulged."

"The evening began with me making a short speech, thanking all of those who had graciously attended, and also our thoughts going out to those who we could not trace. The remainder of the evening was one of exchanging memories of old school days, some happy some sad, as one can expect."

"Then around 10 PM a crowd of us were saying our goodbyes, wishing each other a safe journey home, when I turned towards my good friend Sarah who was standing on the edge of the crowd, and she gave me such a lovely smile."

Agnes's voice drifted away as she pulled out a tissue from the box on the side table. Chris noticed that DC Evans, who had been busy taking notes, took a deep breath at the same time dropping his head lower towards his notepad.

"Sorry once again inspector, I do apologise."

Chris nodded.

"Well anyway, Sarah's smile suddenly began to drain away and she opened her mouth as if to say something, then her head just sank and disappeared from view among the crowd. Then everything seemed to descend into utter confusion. An ambulance was called for, and they immediately took poor Sarah away to the hospital."

"Then this morning I received a phone call from the police who informed me that Sarah was dead and that you would be contacting me to request a statement regarding the events of last night, and quite naturally I have been worried ever since."

"Agnes, can you cast your mind back to when you said Sarah smiled at you. Did she react as if someone had pushed or bumped into her?"

Agnes let her mind drift back before answering Chris.

"Yes, now I remember, her head just for a split second seemed to give a barely visible shake, then she was gone. That's all I can recall."

"And prior to or just before you noticed that, did you hear anything or notice anyone behaving in a strange way?"

"No," Agnes replied.

Lastly, Chris showed her the sketch of the old lady, but Agnes said that she had no recognition of her. Chris and DC Evans spent the next thirty minutes covering a few minor details, before thanking Agnes for her patience. As they prepared to leave, Agnes insisted on walking down the driveway with them to their car. On reaching the car she turned to Chris: "Inspector, have they said how Sarah died? Apart from an announcement of her death on the local news, we have heard nothing."

"I am sorry Agnes, but at this stage in our enquiries I am not allowed to disclose any details."

Then a slightly worried look crossed her face.

"Oh, I have just remembered, I hope someone is taking care of Sarah's dog Poppy, it must be so lonely now she is gone."

"I am sure that has all been arranged," Chris replied in a reassuring voice.

"She just had the one pet, a dog?" he continued. "Not a cat?"

"Definitely not," replied Agnes sternly. "She could not abide them; they were forever scratching up the plants in her garden."

Agnes then thanked them both for their kindness and understanding before turning and making her way back up the driveway.

No Further Progress

Back at the police station, Chris reported his findings to Chief Inspector Norris who decided that because of the number of possible witnesses involved he would assign one extra officer to the investigation, a DC Bruce Hobbs. He also informed Chris that due to the urgency of the investigation it would be necessary to work the weekend.

The next morning, Friday, Chris arrived early at his office. While awaiting the arrival of DC Evans and Hobbs, he began compiling details on a display board of how the deaths of Tommy Anderson and Sarah Middleton might be related.

"Come in," called out Chris, in response to a knock at his office door.

The door opened and in strode DC Hobbs, an officer who always wore a permanent smile, even in moments of adversity. He was in his early thirties, over six foot tall, a dedicated officer who had passed over the opportunity of promotion several times, simply because he did not like being placed in a position where he would be compelled to instruct others what they had to do. The reason, he explained, was the result of spending six years in the army prior to joining the police force.

"Good morning, DC Hobbs. Please take a seat," said Chris, before handing him two folders, each one containing details of the deaths of Tommy Anderson and Sarah Middleton.

Five minutes later DC Evans arrived in the office. Chris gave the two detectives fifteen minutes to briefly study the notes concerning the two cases.

"Now gentlemen," Chris began. "Because of the nature in which these two victims were killed, it appears that these two crimes could be closely linked, and you will find I have highlighted the main points in the reports. As you can see on the display board these two victims do not seem to be related in any way, their ages are vastly different, the only two things which seem to connect them are what was used to kill them, the steel bolts, and that both victims had a great disliking for cats. Any comments?"

"Not really sir," replied DC Hobbs. "All I can say is, whoever did these killings must be a right weirdo."

"I agree," replied Chris, as he handed them each a list of names and addresses of those who were present on the night Sarah Middleton was killed. "So now begins the footslog. I have divided up the names and addresses of all the potential witnesses who were present when Sarah Middleton was killed. And to avoid crossing each other's path, I have tried to divide them into three separate areas of the town. So off we go and good luck. The sooner we find this idiot or idiots the better for everyone!"

The following eleven days of interviewing potential witnesses, however, proved to be fruitless, with no headway being made into the identity of who was responsible for the death of Sarah Middleton. Chris contacted DC's Evans and Hobbs and arranged for them to meet him in his office the following morning, Tuesday.

"Take a seat, gentlemen," said Chris as DC's Evans and Hobbs arrived at his office the following morning.

"First of all let me thank you for your efforts and the miles you have covered in the pursuit of the killer or killers in these crimes. However, it seems our efforts have not uncovered any further clues, so after giving it a lot of thought I think it would be a good idea to go back to the beginning, and delve a little deeper into the killing of Tommy Anderson."

"But sir, don't you think it would be better to concentrate on people from the local area who have a dislike of cats?" asked DC Hobbs.

"Good thinking, Hobbs. But when you take into account how many people out there dislike cats, I don't think their dislike would drive them to go out on a killing spree. I will, however, make a note of your comments just in case we have to follow that line of enquiry."

"Now what I would like you both to do," Chris continued, "is to try and find any family connections between the guests at the reunion and the Anderson family, while I arrange another interview with Tommy Anderson's parents. I know it will be boring sat in front of your computer screens cross-checking family histories, but somewhere in there is the answer we are looking for."

"There is one good piece of news however, Chief Inspector Norris has decided that we do not have to work this weekend. And that for me means barbeque time. Have you two got any plans?"

"I will probably spend the weekend with my brother and his family in Yorkshire," replied DC Evans.

"My wife will make that decision on Friday night sir, so until then I am kept in the dark," laughed DC Hobbs in reply.

As they both departed his office, Chris picked up the phone and dialled the number of Tommy Anderson's parents. Tommy's father answered the call and agreed that it would be convenient for Chris to pay them a visit that same afternoon. On his arrival, Tommy's father Alan greeted him.

"Come in inspector, please come through into the living room. I am happy to say that my wife Anne is feeling much better now, please take a seat."

In the living room Alan's wife Anne, who was watching the television, gave him a warm smile as he sat down at the coffee table.

"Would you like a tea or coffee inspector?" asked Alan.

"Tea would be fine, milk no sugar please."

"Alan," Anne said as she shut off the television. "Let me make the tea for the inspector while you both discuss the investigation into Tommy's death."

The warmth of her smile disappeared as she left the room. Minutes later she returned with the tea for Chris, placed it on the table and then left the room.

"This is a very tough time for us both, inspector. We held Tommy's funeral last week, how we managed to get through the day I just don't know," said Alan. "Hopefully today you have brought us some positive news regarding the investigation into his death."

"I will be quite honest with you, Alan, we do seem to have hit a brick wall regarding the investigation, and that is why I am here today to try and find out if there is any connection between Tommy's death and another killing which happened recently."

"Which killing was that inspector, and why do you think there may be some connection with Tommy's death?"

"All I can tell you at the moment, is that it concerns the death of a Mrs Sarah Middleton who died in similar circumstances whilst attending a reunion at St Hughes comprehensive school."

"Yes I read about that in the local newspaper, but how can that have any connection with the way in which Tommy died?" asked Alan.

"In all honesty, Alan, at this present time I cannot disclose to you any possible connections with the death of Tommy and Mrs

Middleton, but would you have any objections if I ask you a few questions with regards to your family background, or your wife Anne's family background, just in case there might be something hidden away which might connect the two crimes?"

Alan nodded in agreement.

"Well inspector, firstly I have not been completely honest with you regarding my marital status. Anne and I are not married, we are just partners, have been ever since I divorced my wife, Susan. Susan was Tommy's mother. I haven't seen her since we divorced. And the reason for the divorce, well it all stems from the upset caused by Tommy getting that girl pregnant when he was fifteen years old. Susan was a very religious woman and she blamed me for being too lenient with Tommy. And that just about covers my side of the family, I don't have any brothers or sisters and any living relatives that I know of."

Chris was busy noting down all the details as Alan spoke.

"And what about this girl who Tommy got pregnant, can you tell me her name?"

"Yes, her name was Amber Megson."

"And where was this Amber Megson living when she fell pregnant?"

"She lived just three houses away from here. She was a bit of a wild character, just like her mother Joan. I didn't like her, but for some strange reason my wife, sorry partner Anne, were always on very friendly terms with them. And as I told you in my first statement, after the upset of Amber getting pregnant, her and her mother Joan suddenly moved away. Where to I have no idea. Joan had a husband Barry, bit of a strange person, kept himself to himself, never one for mixing with other folks. I think he was employed in some sort of engineering capacity."

Chris looked up from his notebook.

"And I hope you don't think this is rude of me Alan, but as Anne is not here, can you possibly answer questions on her behalf regarding her family background? Would you be happy with that?"

"I do not see a problem with that inspector. Actually there is not very much to tell you about her. We both grew up in the same neighbourhood, went to the same school. She was like me really, had no brothers or sisters or close relatives, her husband died a few years prior to us becoming partners."

"Well thanks for your time, Alan," said Chris as he prepared to leave. "There is just one thing I must ask, when Tommy was having his relationship with Amber Megson, where did they spend most of their time together?"

"Tommy was always at her house, her parents were never at home in the evenings, her mother Joan spent most of her time playing bingo, and as for Amber's father Barry, he was never out of the pub."

"And did the Megson's have a cat?"

"Yes it belonged to Joan, she absolutely doted on it," replied Alan expressing a half-smile.

As Chris climbed into his car he puzzled over why Alan should smile when he was asked about the Megson's cat. Once back at the police station, Chris looked through the folder which contained the names of the guests who had attended the St Hughes school reunion, but there was no mention of the name Megson. It was late Friday afternoon when DC's Evans and Hobbs reported back to Chris that they had not been able to find any family connections between the school reunion guests, and the Anderson family.

R&R Time

It was six o'clock on Friday evening when Dave Evans set off to visit his brother Tony and his partner Patty, along with their two children, William aged eight and John aged six, who lived just outside the town of Malton in Yorkshire. It was a little after seven thirty when he arrived at their converted barn. Within seconds of knocking on their door it was opened by his brother Tony.

"Come in, Dave," he said as he shook Dave's hand. "Give me your bag, you're just in time to sit down for supper."

As Dave entered the dining room, Patty was busy serving up the evening meal to William and John who were seated at the table.

"Good evening, Uncle Dave," they shouted in unison.

"Good evening you guys. It's nice to see you again," responded Dave.

"Hello Dave," said Patty. "How was your journey? I would imagine it was the usual Friday night rush, everyone in a hurry to get home for the weekend."

Dave nodded.

"Now, Dave," she said pointing to a chair. "If you would like to sit here next to Tony, your supper will be on the table in a few seconds."

As Patty placed Dave's supper in front of him she addressed William and John.

"Now just remember you two, I know you are both happy and excited to see Uncle Dave again, but just remember what you promised before his arrival, that you would not begin to ask him any questions until we had all finished our suppers."

Dave looked across at William and John, giving them a wink and a smile. After supper was over, Dave retired into the living room with his two nephews while Tony and Patty tidied up the kitchen. For the next hour it was total excitement for the two boys as they interrogated Dave with numerous questions about his life in the police force, while at the same time showing him their latest electronic games and toys. At 8.30 PM that evening Patty decided that it was bedtime for William and John. Once they were bathed and in their pyjamas it was off to bed, but not before they had delivered their hugs and kisses on Uncle Dave.

"And before you head off to bed," Dave asked them. "What have you boys got planned for me tomorrow?"

"Shooting, we are going to do some shooting, target practice," answered William.

"Oh Dave, I forgot to tell you that I recently bought them each an air rifle, and they cannot wait to show you what fine shots they are," said Tony.

"Okay you boys, give your dad a kiss, then it is off to bed, sleep, and no talking," said Patty with a smile.

"Goodnight, Uncle Dave," they shouted as they raced off to bed. "See you in the morning."

"How are things in the auction business?" Dave asked Tony as he relaxed back into the settee.

Tony was an auctioneer dealing mainly in agricultural sales.

"Just average for this time of the year," replied Tony. "And how are things in the police force? I can only imagine that trying to solve crime is a never ending task."

Dave nodded in agreement before replying.

"Although for obvious reasons I can't disclose any details of the current case I'm working on but at this moment in time we are completely baffled as to what particular weapon was used to kill two people."

"Sorry Dave I shouldn't have asked, you came here for a rest and a change of scenery and what did I do, begin by asking you about your work. Now let me get you a glass of wine, then when Patty comes back we can have a good old gossip, and without a mention of work."

Then along with Patty they spent the rest of the evening chatting about past events until tiredness eventually took its toll and they all retired to bed.

DC Hobbs along with his wife Brenda relaxed in front of the television that Friday night. On the coffee table next to Bruce's armchair stood his favourite tipple, a pint of beer. Although dedicated to his work, he always welcomed a break from chasing the 'scumbags' as he called them, the criminal elements and lowlifes who had no respect for people or property. But as he gazed at the television he couldn't stop his mind drifting back to the killings of Tommy Anderson and Sarah Middleton, and how the killer or killers had silently injected those steel bolts into their victims. His wife Brenda looked across at him and observed that he had a vacant look on his face.

"And what may I ask are you thinking about?" she asked him.

"Oh, nothing really Brenda, just something which I find a bit puzzling."

"Well all I can say is, if it's something associated with work, just let it go because you are on your rest time."

"Yes dear," he replied as he reached out for his pint of beer.

His days off were split between playing golf, gardening, or shopping with Brenda. As tomorrow was a Saturday they had decided to go into town and do their grocery shopping. With the shopping complete they would then have a restaurant lunch, before spending the remainder of the afternoon visiting both of their parents who lived within a short distance of each other.

Brenda made a salad on their return home later that evening which they ate on the picnic table in the garden. That night as they went to bed Bruce was still puzzling over the two killings, and wondering what might provide the final answer.

"Get up, Uncle Dave, it's time for target practice," said William as he and his brother John jumped onto Dave's bed.

Dave blinked his eyes open and looked at the bedside clock which showed seven thirty.

"There is definitely no rest for the wicked," he said. "I come out here into the peace and tranquillity of the countryside for a rest, and what do I get, being woken up by two pesky kids."

"You are not wicked, Uncle Dave," said William with a worried look on his face. "You are fabulous."

"I was only joking William," said Dave, at the same time giving him a hug.

John meanwhile sat on the bed with a puzzled look on his face: "Uncle Dave can I ask you something, what is tranquillity?"

Before Dave could answer there was a knock at the bedroom door and Patty entered the room.

"Now listen you two," she said to the boys. "Your Uncle Dave comes here for a well-earned rest and what does he get? Nothing but disturbance from some wild kids!"

"That's just what Uncle Dave said Mum, but we love him," they both shouted.

After breakfast, and with what looked like being a perfect day with the sun shining, Uncle Dave was led outside by two excitable boys to begin a morning of target practice. Firstly, Dave insisted on them learning the rules of gun safety. William and John both sat down on the grass and listened intently as he outlined the basic rules of gun safety.

Rule 1 - Never point a gun at anyone, even when it is not loaded.

Rule 2 - Always aim towards the target, and never try loading a pellet into the rifle when it is cocked. If it accidentally fires it could trap your fingers.

Three separate targets were set up on a fence at the bottom of the garden, and with the picnic table as a stable platform from which to shoot from, the competition began. William, being the stronger of the two brothers, did manage the task of cocking his rifle, but John had to rely on the assistance of his uncle. Two hours had passed and nearly a box of pellets had been discharged before tiredness began to take its toll on William and John. Dave's right arm was also beginning to feel sore due to the constant cocking of John's gun. Dave who had been elected as the referee in the shooting competition declared it a draw, although William stated that as he was the eldest he should have been the winner.

The remainder of Saturday soon passed, and after having Sunday lunch with his brother and his family it was time for Dave to begin his journey home. After saying his goodbyes to Tony and his family he set off for home. During his journey he allowed his thoughts to drift back over an idea which had begun the previous day. And as he drew closer to his destination he silently said to himself: Yes, that could be the answer.

The Engineer

DI Chris Knowles arrived early in his office on Monday morning, feeling totally re-energised after spending a relaxing weekend entertaining family and friends at their barbecue on Saturday afternoon. Now it was a return to the task of tackling crime, and the most pressing of all was the investigation into the killings of Tommy Anderson and Sarah Middleton. He took a deep breath as he opened the folders relating to the two killings, drew out their contents and began by trying to make comparisons between the two cases. The clock in his office showed 7.55 AM when DC's Evans and Hobbs walked in.

"Good morning, gentlemen. Please take a seat. I hope you both had a pleasant and restful weekend. Now as you know, our priority is the Anderson and Middleton killings, and I will be the first to admit that I do not have a single clue or idea of where to make our next move to catch those responsible."

He continued, "In the Anderson case however, I do think that the main connection lies between the families of Megson and Anderson. And in the killing of Sarah Middleton there seems to be nothing to connect the two cases, except for both of the victims having a dislike of cats. Do either of you have any thoughts or ideas which may be of help?"

"Well sir," DC Evans replied. "I know this suggestion may sound a little bit far-fetched, but so far we have not been able to figure out what sort of silent weapon was used to fire the steel bolts into the victims."

"And?" Chris asked.

DC Evans then related his experience with his nephews that weekend when they were shooting with the air rifles.

"On the journey back home sir I thought, as an air rifle was pretty well silent would it not be possible to apply the same principle to fire a steel bolt into the victims?"

Chris did not immediately reply to the suggestion from DC Evans, instead he sat down at his desk stroking his chin with his left hand, as if deep in thought.

"Yes DC Evans, that is a possibility worth considering, you might just have a point."

"Now," Chris continued. "Today I am going to try and trace the whereabouts of a Mr Barry Megson and his wife Joan, who hopefully are still living somewhere not too very far away from here. And what I would like you two gentlemen to do is go back through the list of guests who attended the school reunion, and find out what their names were before they were married, and if there is anyone with a connection to a Mr Barry Megson."

As DC Evans and DC Hobbs departed his office, Chris switched on his computer and logged onto the council electoral register for the local area. However, the Megson's it seemed had chosen not to be on the public list of voters, so Chris was obliged to apply direct to the council for their address. Listed as living at the address, 31 Connell Street were a Mr Barry Megson, Mrs Joan Jones, Amber Megson, and a Miss V Megson. Miss V Megson thought Chris, that would probably be Tommy Anderson's daughter. Chris made a note in his notebook of the address where the Megson's lived, 31 Connell Street, a not so very nice district of the town. And as a precaution Chris decided to take DC Hobbs with him on the visit. He also instructed DC Hobbs not to mention anything regarding the death of Sarah Middleton.

Pulling up outside the address they were both surprised to find that it was a clean, well-presented semi-detached house with a well-kept garden. The other houses in the street, by comparison, were a complete shambles with rubbish strewn around them. Within seconds of ringing the door bell, the door opened and they were confronted by a short, powerfully built old man, who Chris guessed was Barry Megson.

"What do you want?" he asked, at the same time giving them both a hard look.

Chris introduced himself and DC Hobbs, before explaining that they were looking into the death of Tommy Anderson and perhaps he could help in their enquiries.

"And what the hell has his death got to do with me or my family?" Barry Megson replied, his voice rising in anger.

"Well Mr Megson, I have reason to believe that you were once near neighbours of the Anderson family, and as such may hold some valuable clues which may help to advance our investigation."

Perhaps it was the way in which Chris chose his words, but Barry Megson's attitude suddenly softened into a friendlier manner.

"I suppose you had better come inside then. Go through into the living room, that's straight ahead, then on the left."

He followed them through into the living room where he invited them to take a seat. Chris immediately complemented him on the décor of the living room, which brought a look of pride to Barry's face.

"Yes," Barry replied proudly. "I did all the decorating myself, and everything you see in this house is all paid for, we do not owe a penny to anyone."

"Mr Megson, Barry. Do you mind if I call you Barry?" Chris asked. "As I said earlier, DC Hobbs and I are trying to establish the facts into the death of Tommy Anderson who died in very strange circumstances earlier this year."

At the mention of Tommy Anderson's name Barry's expression once again changed to one of anger.

"Inspector, do you have to mention the name of Tommy Anderson? Do you know what that ba----- did to my fifteen-year-old daughter? He got her pregnant!"

DC Hobbs who was taking notes looked nervously across at Chris as Barry clenched his fists in anger.

"Barry, I do apologise. I did not intend to cause you any upset, and I will try not to refer to him again. And how did your wife take the news when she found out your daughter was pregnant?" Chris asked.

"Not good, that's why we moved out here. My wife felt a sense of shame, it affected her health, mentally."

"I am sorry to hear that Barry, really sorry. And your daughter, is she doing okay?"

At the mention of his daughter it brought a smile to Barry's face.

"She had a little girl who is now fourteen years old, Vanessa is her name. She lives with her mother Amber in Colchester."

"And your wife Barry, what is her name?"

The question instantly brought a scowl to Barry's face, his fists clenching once again.

"Barry I do apologise once again, but I am obliged to ask certain questions even though you may find some of them a little painful."

"Joan, her name is Joan! And while we are on the subject of my wife her name is Joan Jones and not Joan Megson, she decided to keep her maiden name when we married." Barry replied angrily. "Now can you get on with your questions and leave us in peace. And before you ask, she is not at home, she is out walking. She spends most of her time walking, ever since some evil bas---- shot her cat five years ago! That cat was the love of her life, and its death finally drove her over the edge. The experts tell us that she will never recover mentally."

"And one final question I must ask Barry. Since you moved away from your last address in Briar Avenue have you ever been back there or had any contact with anyone in that area?"

The expected outburst of anger never came from Barry, instead he gave a half-smile and a confident reply.

"No."

"Well Barry, I think that is all the questions I need to ask and I would like to thank you for your co-operation."

As Chris and DC Hobbs stood up to leave Chris commented on the neatness of Barry's garden, and asked him if gardening was his hobby.

"No, certainly not," Barry replied. "My main hobby is spending time in my workshop, I love making and repairing things. Around this area I am known as Mr Fix It. All of my working life was spent in mechanical engineering repairing machinery."

"Would you like to see my workshop?" he said, his face now beaming with pride.

"Yes please, Barry."

"Follow me, the workshop is outside in what was once the garage."

Chris and DC Hobbs followed Barry out through the rear door of the house. Unlocking the garage door, he stepped inside followed by Chris and DC Hobbs.

"Please, come in. As you can see I have two lathes, one for turning wood, another for metal; a welding machine, in fact I have all the tools necessary for many repair jobs, but the one thing I really enjoy doing is designing and developing ideas."

"Barry I am impressed by the layout of your workshop, and the effort you have put into it. You deserve to be proud of it."

"Do you do plumbing as well?" Chris asked as he observed various sizes of plastic tube stacked in a corner of the workshop.

For a few seconds Barry hesitated in his response to Chris's question.

"Not really, well perhaps occasionally. Oh, you noticed the plastic pipes, I used those for one of my experiments."

"And if you take my advice Barry, whatever you do, don't ever tell anyone what you invent or design."

Barry's demeanour, which had slumped briefly when Chris mentioned the plastic pipes, quickly returned after Chris offered his advice. Chris then decided that it was time to leave.

"Barry I would like to thank you for your help and hospitality," Chris said, at the same time offering his hand, which Barry accepted and shook warmly.

A look of relief appeared to cross Barry's face as Chris and DC Hobbs said their goodbyes and returned to their car.

"He is hiding something sir, he is a nasty piece of work. I would not like to get on the wrong side of him," DC Hobbs said.

"I agree, DC Hobbs. We will have to dig a little deeper into his background, but what puzzled me most was his brief loss of confidence when I mentioned those plastic pipes and plumbing. But that, DC Hobbs, is the art of detective work, ask the most obscure questions and sometimes it can bring out the answers to a crime."

The Gardeners

Back at the police station Chris arranged for a meeting that afternoon with DC Evans and DC Hobbs.

"Now, DC Evans, hopefully you have managed to uncover a few clues from your task of trawling through the marriage records of the ladies who attended the St Hughes school reunion."

"Yes sir. There was only one person on the list of guests who had any connection to a family by the name of Megson, and that was a Mrs Joan Jones," DC Evans replied.

"And what is the address of this Megson family? And what is the Christian name of Mr Megson?" Chris asked.

DC Evans did a quick scan of his paperwork before answering.

"A Mr Barry Megson of 31 Connell Street, who married a Miss Joan Jones 32 years ago."

"Now perhaps we might begin to join up the dots," Chris said in a more confident voice. "But the only connection so far between the Anderson and Megson families is the instance of Tommy Anderson getting Amber Megson pregnant, and I can't see anyone committing murder for that, even though there are some very strange people in today's society," Chris said.

"But when we interviewed Alan Anderson he told us that he had no idea where the Megson family had moved to. And he also appeared not to have any interest in where they had moved to," DC Evans replied.

"Yes, I agree," said Chris. "Any more thoughts or ideas, DC Hobbs?"

"Well sir, moving back to the start of these two killings the dislike of cats seems to be one of the main themes, just what if Tommy Anderson had found out where the Megson family had moved to and decided to seek revenge on them for taking his daughter away from him, by shooting Joan Jones's cat."

"And how do you think he found out about where the Megson's lived, apart from accidentally meeting them." Chris asked. "Isn't it just possible that as he was a gardener working for the council he could have seen her when he was working in one of the many parks in the town, and followed her home?"

Chris nodded in agreement: "Yes that could be the answer. So I think our next move will be to contact the council and find out if there were any employees who worked with Tommy Anderson on a regular basis, and if they remembered any instance when Tommy may have met Joan Jones."

"DC Evans can you phone the council parks department and ask them if they still have any employees who worked with Tommy Anderson on a regular basis? But moving along a bit further down the line I still do not see any connection between the killing of Tommy Anderson and Sarah Middleton."

"Sir."

"Yes, DC Evans."

"I nearly forgot, when I was looking for any connections in the two cases I went back through the addresses of the people who were invited to the St Hughes school reunion and the address given for Mrs Joan Jones was the same address as Sarah Middleton, 21 Calver Street."

For a few seconds Chris stared open-mouthed.

"And yet Agnes Forbes who organised the reunion was so certain that she had recorded accurately all of the details of those who attended. How could she give two different people the same address?"

"DC Hobbs, while DC Evans is contacting the council, you and I will pay another visit to Agnes Forbes to try and find out why these two people had the same address. I will also give myself a slap on the wrist for not spotting this earlier."

Thirty minutes later they arrived at Agnes Forbes address.

"Please come in inspector, and this gentleman is?"

"Oh so sorry, Agnes. I would like you to meet DC Hobbs, a valuable member of the police force."

"Please take a seat. Would you both like a coffee or tea?"

"Coffee would be fine thank you," Chris replied.

Minutes later she returned with the cups of coffee.

"I must ask you inspector, are you making any progress into the investigation of poor Sarah Middleton's death?"

"Yes we are, Agnes, but very slowly."

"We have come to see you today because in the details which you gave us regarding the guests who were invited to the school reunion, there were two people who had the same address, and we were hoping you could tell us if a mistake had been made when you compiled the guest list."

"Can you please show me the list, inspector?

Chris passed her the folder, which she opened and began to look down the guest list.

"Yes of course, here it is inspector, Sarah Middleton and Mrs Joan Jones of 21 Calver Street. I can explain what happened. When I was compiling the guest list I could not find the address for Joan Jones until I spoke to Sarah Middleton who knew where Joan lived. And as I had nearly reached the deadline for sending out the invitations, Sarah agreed that she would send out the invitation to Joan Jones on my behalf, using her own home address as RSVP. I hope that will be of assistance, inspector."

"Yes that is excellent, Agnes, another box ticked as they say."

Chris drank the remainder of his coffee and stood up to leave.

"I hope you don't think it rude of me to be dashing off, Agnes, but it is very important that we at the police station insert another piece into the jigsaw of this case."

"Inspector, you do not have to apologise, I fully understand your position," Agnes replied as she shook hands with Chris and DC Hobbs.

Back at the police station, DC Evans was waiting with the good news that the council gardeners who worked with Tommy

Anderson would be available for an interview tomorrow morning. The following morning, Chris along with DC Hobbs and DC Evans drove to a suburb of town known as Rookery Fields where one of three council gardening crews would be working, the same gardening crew who Tommy Anderson last worked for.

Chris identified himself to the gardening foreman, a Mr Alan Hutchinson, and explained the reason for his visit, stating that he would require a statement from everyone who had had a close working relationship with Tommy Anderson.

"I can save you a lot of time in that respect, inspector."

"That bloke over there, John Shaw is his name, just tell him that I have said it is okay for you to talk to him," he said, pointing to a distant figure that could be seen chopping away at some bushes.

"Thank you, Mr Hutchinson."

John Shaw stopped chopping away at the bushes as Chris and his colleagues walked up.

"Good morning Mr Shaw, sorry to interrupt you. I am Detective Inspector Christopher Knowles and these are my colleagues DC Evans and DC Hobbs. We are investigating the death of Tommy Anderson and we believe that you were a close workmate of his."

"Yes, I worked with Tommy for at least the last ten years, a really good mate, one of the best," replied John Shaw.

"Did he ever talk about his daughter?"

"All the time inspector, and his bitterness towards Joan Megson for taking his daughter away. Joan Megson even stopped Amber Megson from having contact with Tommy."

"And how do you know this if Tommy didn't know where Joan Megson lived."

"Well, he bumped into Joan Megson a few months ago when we were working in Eagle Park. I was there and what a set-to they had, she was like an absolute maniac. But Tommy really lost his cool with her when she told him that, as long as she was alive, Tommy would never see his daughter."

"And did Tommy make any physical threats to Joan Megson?"

"No, but the last thing that he did to her was point his finger directly into her face and say, 'I will fix you, you cat loving bitch'. What he meant by that I have no idea, but Tommy was raging for the rest of the week."

"You have been most helpful, Mr Shaw," Chris said as he shook his hand. "I will not detain you any longer."

On the drive back to the police station Chris decided to stop off for a brief visit to Tommy Anderson's father, Alan.

"Come in, inspector. Have you made any progress in the investigation?"

"Sorry, Alan, I cannot stop. I just wish to ask you, did Tommy ever own a gun, an air rifle?"

"Yes he did until a few months ago. I made him get rid of it, I didn't like it, dangerous things."

"And do you know where he got rid of it?"

"Not really, he probably sold it to one of his mates."

"Oh you asked how the investigation was going, well it seems to be gaining momentum," Chris replied.

A Possible Weapon?

Thanking him Chris set off back to the police station, where that afternoon he convened a meeting with his two DC's to discuss in detail all of the information relating to the two cases.

"Now let's begin," Chris said, pointing to the display board which carried all of the information regarding the killings of Tommy Anderson and Sarah Middleton. We will first take the killing of Tommy Anderson who was killed by a steel bolt whilst drinking in the Crown and Anchor Pub."

"This steel bolt must have been fired into him by a very silent and powerful weapon, because no one heard a shot."

Chris went on, "And in the killing of Sarah Middleton, this was just about identical in detail to the killing of Tommy Anderson, a steel bolt, no sound of a shot, so we can assume that the same weapon was used to fire the steel bolt. All of the possible witnesses were interviewed which drew a blank, apart from the pub landlord, Jack Russell, saying that he had seen a grey-haired old lady carrying a large handbag up close to the victim Tommy, just before he collapsed. A composite sketch was made of this grey-haired old lady, but so far there has been no feedback, she seems to have disappeared."

"An interview with Tommy Anderson's parents also gave us no clues, except for Tommy being a bit of a bully and him having a dislike of cats, there did not appear to be a reason for anyone wanting to kill him. Then three weeks after Tommy Anderson's death, sixty-five year old Sarah Middleton was killed at a school reunion with a very similar steel bolt. Then a small connection between these two deaths came about, whereby it transpired that Sarah Middleton also had a strong dislike of cats."

"And even though we have collected plenty of evidence since then which pulls the two crimes closer together, we are still at a loss as to who the killer or killers might be, and what sort of weapon was used to fire the steel bolts. DC Hobbs what are your thoughts on these crimes, based on the evidence we have collected so far?"

"Well sir, regarding the information that we were given this morning and the possibility that Tommy Anderson did shoot Joan Jones's cat, perhaps it was one of her family members that killed Tommy."

"Yes, I agree that is a possibility," Chris replied. "And that I think is where the final link might lie, with Joan Jones."

"Now let's assume that Tommy Anderson shot and killed Joan Jones's cat, and she got her revenge by killing Tommy," continued DC Hobbs. "Joan Jones, as we know, had an invitation to the reunion at St Hughes School and somehow she found out that Sarah Middleton had a dislike of cats and arranged for her to be killed."

"Yes DC Evans?" prompted Chris.

"Sir, on the subject of what sort of weapon was used in both crimes, I still think that it could be possible to use some sort of air rifle application. After all an air rifle is fairly quiet, and in a crowded atmosphere no one would hear it being fired."

"The problem with that DC Evans," said Chris. "Is that if you walked into a crowded room with an air rifle everyone would see it."

"But not if you slimmed it down sir," DC Hobbs replied.

"Yes, it certainly would need to be slimmed down," Chris responded. "And in my opinion the only way to slim down a gun is to cut the barrel off, and I don't think it would be much use after that."

"Anyway, DC Hobbs, as you are an ex-military man, perhaps you and DC Evans could get your heads together and devise a weapon that could be capable of firing a steel bolt."

"Sir, one last thing. This grey-haired old lady who so far no one has recognised from the composite sketch. Even though this person was possibly using some sort of disguise, especially the grey hair, wouldn't you think that someone from the victims' families and witnesses would have recognised something about her?" DC Evans asked.

"Yes, I agree," Chris replied. "That sketch was shown to all the people who had any connection with these two crimes, be it families or witnesses that I showed it to, that is -."

Chris's words tailed off as a sudden frown formed on his face.

"That is except for Anne Anderson and Joan Jones. And it was I who missed them, what a fool I have been. And the reason for that was, Joan Jones was out walking and Anne Anderson excused herself midway through my visit to their house. And so that means another visit to the Anderson and Megson households."

"And as DC Hobbs will probably agree with me, I do not relish another visit to Barry Megson's house. However, if you two can complete your reports, I will make arrangements for those visits. And as I said earlier, can you get your heads together and try to design a weapon that would be capable of firing a steel bolt."

The following morning Chris arranged yet another visit to Alan and Anne Anderson's house. Upon arrival he was greeted by Alan who invited him inside.

"Take a seat, inspector. Would you like a tea or coffee?"

"Coffee would be fine thank you, Alan," replied Chris.

Anne was sat on a lounge chair watching the television as Chris entered the living room, giving him just a brief smile she returned her gaze back to the television as if in a trance. Minutes later Alan returned with a coffee for Chris.

"Now inspector, how is the investigation going? Hopefully you will have some good news for us."

"Yes Alan, we are making steady progress, but first there are just a few things that need to be cleared up to enable us to move forward. When I conducted my first interview with you and your wife Anne, do you remember me showing you that composite sketch of an old lady who we thought could possibly have some connection to our investigation?"

"Yes I do. inspector, but as I remember I did not recognise her."

"Well this is the reason for my visit today, because I don't believe I showed it to Anne."

"That is correct, inspector. If I recall she was very upset at that time and she left the room. Do you have the sketch with you please?"

Chris took the sketch from his briefcase and handed it to Alan who approached his partner Anne.

"Anne dear, the inspector would like you to take a look at this sketch and see if you recognise the person on it."

Chris closely studied Anne's face as she averted her gaze from the television and looked at the sketch which Alan handed to her. In an instant a look of shock flashed briefly across her face, before tears welled up in her eyes. She then reached out and pulling a tissue from a nearby box began dabbing away her tears.

"Anne, did you recognise the person in the sketch?" asked Alan.

Anne did not answer, instead she just shook her head, got up from her lounge chair, and through her tears apologised to Chris and left the room.

"Inspector, what can I say," Alan said. "Do you think that Anne possibly recognised the person in sketch?"

"It is difficult to say Alan, the shock of losing someone can leave emotional scars for a long time. I apologise for the upset it caused her, but it was necessary that she saw the sketch, and I hope that she soon feels better."

Chris drank the remainder of his coffee and stood up to leave. Placing the sketch back in his briefcase, he shook Alan's hand, thanking him for his patience and drove back to the police station. Back at the police station he immediately went to the office occupied by DCs Evans and DC Hobbs, who were huddled over a series of drawings.

"Gentlemen, I believe we are getting closer to finding out who our mystery old lady is, because I think that Anne Anderson recognised her."

"And," DC Hobbs said giving a broad smile. "We think that we have solved the design of the weapon that was used to deliver the steel bolts. Do you remember sir when Barry Megson was showing us his workshop and how he had a love of designing and developing ideas. Well working on the theory by DC Evans that an air rifle system could be used, we have come to the conclusion of how the weapon was made."

He continued, "In Barry Megson's workshop there was a selection of various sizes of plastic pipes which Barry Megson said he used in an experiment. All that would be required would be a spring from an air rifle inserted into a plastic tube, which had one end blanked off, a locking mechanism which held the compressed spring, and a release trigger. Insert the steel bolt in behind the spring, hold it up close to the victim, place a little of your body weight on it and press the trigger."

He handed a drawing of their idea to Chris, who after studying it for a few minutes replied: "Yes, yes of course, DC Hobbs, I am sure you are both correct. Now assuming your theories on the weapon design are correct, and Anne Anderson did recognise the old lady in the sketch, our next move is to ask Joan Megson, or as we now know her - Joan Jones, to take a look at the sketch of the old lady."

"Now this part of the enquiry will need to be conducted with a very delicate approach, because as DC Hobbs will confirm, Barry Megson could be a nasty piece of work. And so I think the best thing for me to do is report our findings to Chief Inspector Colin Norris and decide on a plan for our next move. The other minor problem we have is trying to contact Joan Jones for her to have a look at the sketch of the old lady, because according to her husband Barry she spends most of her time out walking, and it would be senseless for us to drive over to their house if she wasn't home."

Chris left the two detective constable's office and went directly to a meeting with Chief Inspector Colin Norris.

"Good morning sir, hope that you are well," Chris said as he entered Inspector Norris's office.

"Yes thank you, Chris. Please take a seat. And I hope that you have some good news to tell me regarding your investigation into the murders of Tommy Anderson and Sarah Middleton."

Chris then spent the next hour discussing all of the evidence that had been collected regarding the two murders.

"Yes I think you are on the right track, Chris, and I agree with you that Barry Megson could be a nasty piece of work, so we will have to tread very carefully. Now with regards to the problem of making sure that Joan Jones will be at home when you call to show her the sketch of the old lady, I think I have the perfect answer, I can pretty well guarantee that she will be home tomorrow."

"You can sir, how is that?"

"Tomorrow the weather forecast is for an absolute downpour all day, some areas could even be flooded, and there are not many people who enjoy walking in a heavy downpour. I can arrange for a uniformed backup team to be on standby for you tomorrow morning Chris, you just tell me what time you will need them, then fingers crossed this enquiry can be brought to a conclusion."

"Yes sir, thank you."

Chris returned to his office, and after a discussion with his two detective constables decided that they would arrive at the Megson's house at nine o'clock tomorrow morning. As Chris and DC Hobbs had previously visited the Megson's house he made the decision that DC Evan's would remain in the car. Chris then informed Chief Inspector Norris of the time and place that the uniformed backup team would be required.

The Visit

The following morning, as predicted by Inspector Norris, the downpour arrived. With the rain lashing down, Chris along with his two DC's set off for the Megson's house. There was a police car containing four uniformed officers parked just around the corner as they turned into Connell Street. Before exiting the car outside 31 Connell Street, Chris and DC Hobbs switched on their radio communications, ensuring that the uniformed backup team were in full contact with them. The rain was still pouring down as they walked up the garden path towards the front door of the Megson's house.

Chris rang the doorbell and cursed to himself as the rain poured down soaking through his coat. DC Hobbs was faring no better, a look of absolute despair etched on his face. Chris soon lost his patience when on ringing the doorbell for a third attempt there was still no response, and chose instead to bang heavily on the door with his fist. They then heard a male voice call out from inside the house, "Come in."

Chris immediately felt a sense of danger, and giving DC Hobbs an apprehensive look opened the door and stepped inside. Once inside Chris motioned for DC Hobbs to quietly close the door. However, the sound from the door latch as the door closed brought another response from the direction of the living room, this time it was a female voice.

"We are in the living room, can you please wipe your feet, and then come through and take a seat."

"Yes," Chris replied. "We will be with you in a moment."

Chris, followed by DC Hobbs, cautiously entered the living room. Barry Megson lay on the settee shaking violently, his left leg was covered in congealed blood, from what seemed to be a wound in his thigh. His face had also suffered injury from a heavy blow. Tied to a chair was his wife Joan, whose face was heavily bruised, and had, it seemed, a broken nose. A gag was tied tightly over her mouth. Standing behind her was Anne Anderson, holding a knife to Joan's throat. She also held a short plastic tube to Joan Anderson's left temple.

"Well, what have we here? Why none other than the police to bear witness to a bit of good old-fashioned justice. Please take a seat gentlemen, and do not even try to touch your radios, because I can assure you that I will slice open the throat of this bitch of a killer if you do."

"Sit down!" she shouted. "Now!"

Chris and DC Hobbs did as she requested, at the same time exchanging knowing glances at the sight of the plastic tube held in Anne's hand.

"Do you know what this is?" she shouted loudly, waving the plastic tube in the air. "This is the weapon made by that evil excuse of a man, to kill two innocent people, simply because they did not like cats. Well he found out this morning what it was like to be on the receiving end of his weapon, because I put one of the steel bolts into his leg. Didn't I, Barry?" she said mockingly.

"And this thing in front of me is the evil bitch who killed my beautiful stepson," Anne's hand trembled with rage as the knife blade squeezed tighter onto Joan's throat and blood began to trickle down her neck. It was at this point that Chris attempted to intervene.

"How did you fi-," he began to say.

Anne Anderson immediately told him to be quiet.

"I will do the talking inspector; I am in charge here," she shouted. "How did I find out who killed my stepson Tommy and Sarah Middleton? When you showed me the sketch of the old lady, I knew who it was, even though it was obvious she was wearing a wig and glasses to disguise her identity."

"And how did I find out where this evil couple lived? She continued. "The truth is I have always known where they lived, because their daughter Amber always kept in touch with me, which we kept a secret between the two of us. Even my husband Alan didn't know. Nor does he know that this evil bitch sat before you is my cousin. What a proud moment for me when I found out she is a murderess!"

Anne was on a roll now, "And the other thing that you are dying to ask inspector is how I found out that Joan had killed Sarah Middleton. That was so easy, because I beat it out of her. Unluckily for these two I arrived early this morning. Barry was still in bed when I persuaded Joan to tell me all of their wicked secrets, and as you can see, the rest is history."

"And," she said waving the plastic tube in the air. "I must congratulate Barry on designing such a deadly weapon, he is an absolute genius. When I held it to his leg and fired it, it just went click."

Anne then held the plastic tube against Joan's neck.

Click.

Coffin Time

Here I am laid in my box
In best suit, tie and socks.
They've come to view me now I have gone,
Wondering where my monies gone.

For I did die one week ago
So now they put me out on show,
And as they line up for a peek
Boy they have a bloody cheek!

It is buried in a box
Not where they thought, in my socks.
Will they find it? I don't care.
In the loft or in a chair?

First in line is cousin Dick,
To look at him would make you sick,
Bent and stooped with double chin,
Measly face and oh, so thin.

Next came his wife, a wrinkled crone,
She should really be in a home,
Not for old folks that's a fact,
More like a home for fat old cats!

My neighbour Stan stared down at me,
Thinking my God, where can it be?
But it is a secret I will keep.
Is it shallow or is it deep?

Church Warden Bill he is so fat,
Free meals we can put down to that.
For funerals will guarantee
Sandwiches and a cup of tea.

The coffin moved as he leaned over,
With a face like my dog Rover.
He moved along as he was bid.
Nudged out the way by dear old Syd.

Syd thought he was a smart old chap
Till he wed Rose and got the clap!
On their wedding she looked a honey,
But she only wed him for his money!

Now he's broke without a cent,
All worn out old and bent.
But Rose hangs on with hopes so high,
With me now gone will I supply?

Someone like her without a soul
You wouldn't touch with a ten-foot pole!
Of one thing that you can be sure
Rose will end up very poor!

They kept on filing past so slow,
Until it came to Aunty Flo,
With her low-cut dress showing every bit
Of her looks and ready wit.

Finally, they'd all gone past,
The vicar he was very last,
Looking tall and so devout
Without this time his hand held out.

Wait a moment, who is this
Dressed like she is on the piste?
Well, damn me, if it isn't Gill,
She has turned up with the will!

It's much too late my darling, Gill,
You can forget that stupid will.
For all that time I was with Dot,
We went and spent the bloody lot!

So put the lid upon my box,
Try not to ruffle my best socks,
I leave this life without a care
With two fingers in the air!

The Burial

The lid is on the coffin, I'm wheeled into the hearse,
People they are crying, they cannot find my purse.
They've dug around my garden looking for the loot
But all they found was a tatty boot!

People they all gather round waiting for the cars.
"Over here, over here, that one must be ours."
Rose and Syd climbed aboard for my final trip,
Cousin Dick he was there, not one to miss a trick.

Everyone was crying as they rode along.
Aunty Flo suggested that they sing a song.
"What will we sing about?" interrupted Syd.
Rose said, "Hallelujah, now that he is dead."

So they sang with gusto, clapping full of joy,
Thinking of my money that they would enjoy.
But they must remember, even though I'm dead
The contents of the will have not yet been read.

Arriving at the church there stood Warden Bill,
Big belly was protruding, soon be time to fill.
The vicar he came forward looking so devout,
Looking very saintly with his hand held out.

Crossed himself, eyes aloft, gaze it was so far,
Stepping to the left in front of the second car.
The car did strike him heavily, creating such a din,
Only thing that saved him, he was without sin.

Up rose the vicar angrily, shaking of his fist,
That stupid driver is most definitely drunk.
Syd stepped forward asking everyone for calm
After all the vicar has not come to harm.

The vicar led the way on my final trip
Followed by the mourners a smile upon their lips,
For this moment they hope to savour
Visions of my money could be their next flavour.

O praise the Lord, here our brother lies,
Bow your heads and close your eyes.
We pray his soul is full of grace
For now he goes to a better place.

So they stood, their heads they bowed,
Looking such a solemn crowd.
A eulogy by Rose was read.
Was she happy now I was dead?

With handkerchiefs some dabbed their eyes,
Muffling the sound of their cries.
Others stood, hiding a grin
Thank the Lord we are shut of him!

And so they sang a final hymn,
By now the light was getting dim.
The vicar read a final verse,
Then loaded me into the hearse.

Some wanted me buried in a hole
But I preferred to be burned like coal,
For when I'm ash and in a pot
I'll still be with you miserable lot!

For in my will and to fill their greed,
To share me around they all agreed.
Who'll be first, who can tell?
One thing for sure they'll fight like hell!

They can't read my will for a year
And in this time I've nothing to fear.
They'll spend all their money, push out the boat
While I'm in my pot having a gloat.

Now they've turned me into ash
I'll be treasured just like cash,
Loved and caressed in my pot,
Pity they haven't talked to Dot!

Gone But Not Forgotten

"GOOD MORNING MR Pratt, and how are you on your final day at the office? What is it now 50 years with the company?"

Claude Pratt looked up from the computer screen on which he had been entering details of the company accounts.

"Yes that is correct, Miss Anderson. Times have certainly changed since I began working here as an office boy. There were no computers then, just typewriters and at least twelve people employed doing all the paperwork and accounts."

"Now look at it, here I am office manager, you Miss Anderson my secretary, both of us isolated away from everyone in a nice private office," he went on. "Sometimes life does get a little boring, no more of the old-fashioned office banter any longer."

"Now, now Mr Pratt, do not slip into the doldrums on your last day."

"Yes, Miss Anderson," he sighed.

"And as it is your final day here, can I ask you a favour Mr Pratt?"

"You certainly can, Miss Anderson," Claude replied.

"Will you allow me the pleasure of calling you by your first name, Claude?"

A smile lit up his face and his heart began to beat a little faster.

"That would be absolutely wonderful, Miss Anderson. And can I please call you by your first name, April?"

"Yes."

Claude's eyes turned and followed her as she returned to her desk on the far side of the office. She was a petite slim lady, natural blond, who dressed very modestly. Her age he never knew but he guessed it to be in the region of 45 years. As for her private life, all he knew about her is that she lived alone in a large detached house on the outskirts of town. From the very first day that she began working in his office he felt pangs of desire towards her, but resisted the temptation to broach the subject, after all, he thought, why add more complications to an already miserable married life. Married at twenty-five, his wife Ethel made it quite plain to him that there would be no children in their household, and what she decided was final.

The ticking of the old wooden clock on the office wall interrupted his thoughts. A brief glance at the clock showed it to be three minutes past ten. He loved that old clock, far better than the modern electronic ones. Although the office had been decorated and rearranged many times, he had always insisted that the old clock remained, a little bit of nostalgia.

His mind drifted back to twelve months earlier when he realised that he would soon be retired, with a good company pension, and the drudgery of office work would finally be behind him. What he had not contemplated was the sudden arrival of days-weeks of spare time which he had to fill. Apart from his favourite hobby of stamp collecting nothing else had caused him any interest. Although Ethel was a good wife he shuddered at the thought of spending every minute in the house with her. Now the realisation was beginning to set in. As he tapped away at the computer keyboard he mentally brushed aside the prospect of future boredom, telling himself that he would face that challenge head on when it arrived.

Although his work required absolute concentration he had acquired the skill of being able to enter calculations on the computer while at the same time thinking of past events. Today was one of those days, as he thought back with pride on his rise from being an office boy to office manager in the accounts department at Drakes Engineering. In his early days at Drakes Engineering, and to gain knowledge of the company workings, he voluntarily worked for 2 years with the workers on the production line, where he gained the respect of the workforce for his dedication and hard work. When he next looked up at the clock it showed nearly 12 o'clock, time to head for lunch in the office canteen.

"Miss Anderson, sorry April, time for lunch."

"Yes Claude," she replied, giving him a broad smile.

He opened the office door allowing her to precede him towards the staff canteen, at the same time wondering what sort of reception would greet him from other staff members on this his final day. There was the usual queue waiting to be served at the counter and apart from the usual 'Hello Claude' from several staff and 'how are you?', there was not one mention to him about his final day with the company. The only person to acknowledge and wish him a happy retirement was the lady who served him his soup. Picking up a bread cob and placing it on his tray he followed April across to a vacant table and sat down.

"Miss… sorry April, can I ask you a question? Do you think that I have done anything offensive towards anyone since I stepped into the canteen?"

"I don't think so, not that I noticed. Why do you ask?"

"Well the atmosphere towards me in here is like ice, and not one person has even offered to shake my hand or wish me a happy retirement. I would never for one minute expect to be treated like a celebrity, but a friendly smile would not go amiss."

April placed her cup of tea down in the saucer. Looking at Claude she gave him a warm smile at the same time placing her hand on his.

"I am sure there must be a simple explanation," she replied. "Now enjoy your soup."

He was slightly taken by surprise when her hand touched his, and her reply gave him some reassurance but deep down he felt a sense of betrayal. Finishing his soup, he quickly excused himself and walked slowly back to his office, trying hard to conceal his anger and frustration. At 2 PM that afternoon Claude was still trying hard to contain his hurt feelings towards his colleagues. He was so engrossed in his thoughts he barely noticed April until she was stood up close to him.

"Excuse me, Claude, but I couldn't help noticing how hard today's events have hurt you, and perhaps I could help to make things better if you don't mind me making a bold suggestion."

"No not at all, April."

"Well," she continued. "I never really have any special arrangements for Friday evenings after work, and I was thinking that perhaps as my special treat, you would allow me to take you out for a meal at a very nice restaurant. After all, you have always treated me with the greatest respect and kindness and I would like to return the favour."

Claude began to blush.

"April, that is a very kind and generous offer, but what about my wife? What will people think if I am seen out with another lady? I would lose my good name, be ostracised for life."

"I have already considered the possible consequences," said April. "Let me phone your wife and I will explain to her that you will be a little late getting home, because it is your last day at the company and you have been invited for a meal. Now that is not even a little white lie, wouldn't you agree?"

Claude briefly pondered for a moment.

"Yes, yes that is a very good idea, Miss err, April, very good idea. I will leave it in your capable hands."

Claude's spirits lifted and a rebellious feeling began to rise inside him.

"To hell with those miserable so and so's from the company, I will go and enjoy a meal with April and if anyone does see me with her, see if I care!" he muttered angrily to himself.

Minutes later, April was back by his side.

"Now everything is sorted Claude, I spoke to your wife and she said that would not be a problem and I have booked a table at the Cavalier Restaurant which is about two miles out of town. I also took the liberty, I hope you don't mind, and told them at the restaurant that you would be celebrating your retirement and they offered a free bottle of wine or champagne of your choice."

"Well April, I do not normally drink alcohol, but as this will be a special occasion why not."

A sudden thought crossed his mind: "What about my car, I cannot drink alcohol and drive?" he said to April.

"I have already thought about that Claude, we will leave your car here and take mine. I intend to take good care of you tonight."

A slight feeling of unease crept over him as she gave him a knowing smile before returning to her desk.

It was shortly after 4.30 PM when he shut down his computer for the last time. Ensuring that he had collected all his personal belongings he gave a final glance at the old wooden clock which continued with its steady tick, and followed April out to her car. Apart from a few cleaners in the offices who wished him well, everyone else had already left for home.

As they drove away from the factory, he knew deep down that he was going to miss the 9 AM start of his daily routine.

As they began to reach the outskirts of town into a more affluent area, April pointed out to him a large detached house which stood down a leafy driveway.

"That is where I live Claude, isn't it lovely?"

"Yes, yes it certainly is, and what a wonderful location."

"My father left it to me when he died eight years ago. He worked for the Government up until his retirement. I do sometimes consider selling it and moving to a smaller property as I find it quite large just for myself, but it holds such fond memories."

"If I may ask, April, what was his involvement with the Government?"

"He never really spoke very much about his work, but it did involve a lot of commuting between here and London, and overseas."

Minutes later they arrived outside the Cavalier Restaurant, an old farmhouse which had been restored to its former grandeur. Claude still felt a sense of nervousness as they entered the restaurant. They were greeted by the manager who ushered them to a table in a quiet corner by a window. There were only three other couples in the restaurant, none of whom Claude recognised. He breathed a sigh of relief. A smartly dressed waiter approached.

"Good evening Madam, good evening Sir, I trust you had a pleasant journey."

"Now Sir, I understand this is a very special day for you, and the management has decided that all drinks will be complimentary of the house. If you would like to select something from the drinks menu I will be back shortly to take your order."

Handing them both a menu he left. Claude thanked him, then after a brief look at the wine menu he looked across at April.

"April, as I know very little about wines or alcohol in general what would you recommend I choose?"

"Well from personal experience I would recommend a medium white wine, much easier to consume than a red which tends to be a little heavy on the stomach."

A few minutes later the waiter returned to take their order. Because April was driving she chose spring water. Minutes later the drinks were poured and after a few sips of the wine Claude began to relax, his face taking on a flushed look. For the rest of the evening as they ate they exchanged past experiences of their lives. As the wine relaxed him even further, Claude even went so far as to begin telling April a few risqué jokes. She insisted that she settled the account for the meal, and Claude, who was by this time full of emotion for her, reached over the table and took her hand.

Looking into her eyes with a loving look he said to her: "April, tonight has got to be one of the finest nights of my life, I will treasure this night until the day I die."

"Claude, the night is not over; the best is yet to come."

Her reply had startled him. Had he overstepped the mark? What did she mean? As he eased himself into her car she reached over and secured the seat belt for him, the scent of her perfume further arousing him. It was getting dark as she turned into the driveway leading up to her house. Suddenly realising where they were, Claude began to panic.

"April, what are we doing stopping off at your house? This is not the right thing to do. My wife will be getting worried about me."

Switching off the engine she took hold of his hand.

"Please trust me, Claude, after such a close evening together this, I hope, will be a night to remember, for both of us."

Getting out of the car he followed her up to the house. As she inserted the key in the lock and opened the door he took a deep breath, swallowed hard and followed her inside. His panic by now had subsided and his physical desire for her was beginning to rise. She guided him through into what seemed to be a medium-sized lounge with a thick beige carpet, and a large white soft rug spread in front of an open fireplace. The furniture consisted of a settee and two matching lounge seats, one of which was laid back opposite a large television. Over to the left of the room was a well-stocked bar. As he stood looking around the room trying to absorb the surroundings, April approached him from behind carrying a glass of white wine.

"Claude, please come and sit down over here, on the settee. Sit with me."

As he sat down she handed him the glass of wine, before sitting down beside him.

"Claude, can I ask you, are you happy you came out with me tonight?"

"Yes," he replied, and leaned towards her as if wanting to kiss her. She anticipated his motive and placed her hand on his chest.

"Now Claude, what I want you to do is sit here, relax and enjoy your glass of wine while I go and get ready in the next room, and when you hear me knock on the door it will be the signal for you to come and join me."

Excusing herself she left the room by a door just beyond the bar, closing it gently behind her. After what seemed an age, a knock came on the door. Claude, who had been pacing the floor, downed the remainder of his glass of wine, took a deep breath, strode towards the door, flung it open and stepped inside. His eyes blinked momentarily as the room was in total darkness, except for a single light which was shining on to him from above. Within seconds a blaze of light lit up the room to reveal an audience of all his work colleagues, friends and relations, with his wife at the forefront. What should have been a tumultuous round of applause from this gathering, was replaced with open-mouthed silence as Claude stood there naked, clad only in his socks. A single camera flashed, perhaps taken by an overexcited lady.

Happiness

Happiness is a golden gift, one which we all desire.
If this is not a given gift, how do we acquire?
Through good thoughts and helping hand
Directed towards our fellow man.
No malice in deed, work or toil,
Be of good heart, body and soul.
Rise in the morning bearing a smile,
Your well-being rejoices, bearing no bile.
Diligence, dedication in your daily tasks,
Doing whatever requests you are asked.
If anyone chides or is foul in remark,
Respond with a smile removing their dark.
For at days' end when ready for sleep
We can rest in peace and good thoughts we keep.

My Wife

I never argue with my wife even when she's sweet,
One thing is for certain, she never will be beat.
But I have one advantage which is very clear,
To have the final word by saying "Yes dear."
It took many years of practice to really learn my place,
Doing things correctly, and at the proper pace.
"Are you going to fill the kettle?" she did request of me.
What she really meant to say, "Make me a cup of tea."
But subterfuge and craft is a lethal tool
Woven to achieve, not make me look a fool.
Treading carefully, she moves using every little ploy,
Stringing me along like a little boy.
It's not that I am stupid or without a brain,
But I have to follow orders, and there she goes again.
Driving into town, looking where to park.
"Don't park here, park over there," came the usual bark.
"Yes dear," I complied, as I stared ahead.
I dare not disagree as it's better live than dead.
"You've not parked very straight," came her vocal view.
I've been driving forty years, still don't have a clue!
The next day started brightly as every day it should,
My wife her usual self, slowly drawing blood.
Bread and jam for breakfast and a cup of tea.
Read my daily paper, as quickly as could be
For the airborne tension told me that she would decide
Whether I'd go out or if I stayed inside.

Then the order came, which my happy thoughts did taint:
"Open up that tin, we are going to paint"
"Yes dear," I agree as I gave a little nod.
Her demeanour could be worse than the wrath of God.
And so it was decided that my day was sorted,
Freedom was no more, once again I'm thwarted.
The time it went so quickly as I slapped on the paint,
"I've finished dear; can I go?" "No you flippin aint."
"You've missed a piece over there." Worry crossed my brow,
Standing to attention, didn't dare to have a row.
Finally, inspection time as she strode into the room.
Would I pass this time or face a night of doom?
Tutting rather loudly, she said I'd passed the test.
"Now you can tidy up, no time for a rest!"
"Your tea is on the table, eat it while it's hot."
"Yes dear," as I sat, she doesn't miss a shot.
The meal was finally eaten, now we could retire
To sit and watch the telly, while warming by the fire.
But my day has not yet ended, for she's as smooth as silk.
As I stand to stretch my legs, "Get me a glass of milk!"
I follow orders muttering underneath my breath,
Hope she doesn't hear or she'd demand my death!

Now it's half past ten, days end is drawing near.
"Don't be late coming to bed." "Yes dear!"

*Whoever reads this will probably (hopefully) have the greatest
sympathy for me as the above is only two days out of the year.*

Forgiveness?

SHE STARED INTO the darkness, but still the torment tore at her as she mentally tried to justify the act she was about to embark on. But turning back now would be an act of cowardice. The tears which had trickled down her cheek into the corner of her mouth leaving a salty taste had ceased, her bodily tension slowly draining as if rising from a deep cold pool into the warmth of a summer's day.

Monday morning, another busy day thought Diane. Turning the radio on for the 7 AM news, but not so loud as it was much too early for her son Andrew to be getting ready for school. He would be 8 years old next week, she thought, and apart from the odd disagreement and tantrum he was a joy to have around the house. Diane was 29 years old, and like a few of her friends she had gone through the experience of falling in love and getting pregnant, with Andrew's father then deserting her when he was most needed. But with determination and support from her parents she had built her own secure niche in life for Andrew and herself. A glance at the kitchen clock showed 7.30 AM.

"Andrew, time to get ready for school," she shouted.

Andrew appeared as if by magic, immaculately dressed.

"Hi Mum, can I have toast for breakfast?"

Diane pretended to jump in surprise at his sudden appearance: "Yes of course you can," she replied, at the same time putting the bread into the toaster.

She would drop Andrew off at school by 8.45 AM then continue on to work at the local council until 5.00 PM. Diane's friend, Pat, would collect Andrew from school in the afternoon and care for him until Diane's return.

Parking her car a few hundred yards from the school gates, she gently held Andrew's hand as she walked him towards the pedestrian crossing, as she had done every day since his very first day of school. Ensuring that the traffic was slowing down approaching the pedestrian crossing, she kissed Andrew, who turned and stepped onto the pedestrian crossing. The loudness of a car engine caused Diane to briefly avert her gaze from Andrew's cheery smile as he half turned midway over the crossing.

The car that struck Andrew didn't stop. As a shocked silence descended on the scene, Diane's inner strength drained and she sank slowly down until being held by a comforting passer-by. Her son's prostrate mangled body was attended to by a fast-responding medical team, but their efforts were in vain.

Diane's world passed into a blur except for Andrew's funeral. The driver of the car was eventually traced and arrested. Given a derisory sentence he would be free in 18 months. Diane eventually returned to work which helped to lift the pain of her son's death. Her son's killer was duly freed. She later learned from friends that her son's killer drank late into the night every Friday at a local pub.

Her car moved forward gathering pace, the anger now in her right foot. Headlights off, onto the pavement, so close now, and as her son's killer turned she stared into the darkness.

The Queue

Standing here in a line,
Yawning, blinking, passing the time.
Life is passing, blood pressure high,
Once again another loud sigh.

Got here early, or so I thought,
Try to avoid getting fraught.
Other people all thought the same,
One step ahead, that's the name of the game.

How long have you been in the queue?
Much more than a minute or two?
Yes, I have, you see him at the front,
Since I arrived his head's grown a plant.

And so we stand and we do wait,
Some upright, others not so straight.
Shuffle my feet, fidget and fret
Should I shout, is it my turn yet?

What's that smell, is it him?
Can't be her she's clean and slim.
Purse my lips, create a grin,
Spittle dribbles down my chin.

Look at her, she thinks she's the part,
Nothing but a long-legged tart!
Flaunting herself, so full of lust.
How did she manage to grow such a bust?

A number is called, forward we step,
Movement is painful, that is my hip.
People complain, moan and gripe.
To some it's just like riding a bike.

"Can I have this mum?" "No, you cannot,
Any more and you'll get a swat."
She looked young, so full of youth
But as a mother very uncouth.

Two women talking ever so loud,
Some of their language is very lewd.
Their private lives it doesn't matter,
Life to some is all idle chatter.

A glance at the time, an hours elapsed
Since arriving here behind an old chap.
Should I ask him how old he is
Or remain silent avoiding a quiz?

Choosing the latter was my choice,
Rather than an offending voice.
This is so boring, but what can I do?
Spending so long in a post office queue!

Bert

Friday Night, Saturday Morning

"PLEASE HURRY UP and open the door, Gwyneth," Bert muttered to himself. "This is the last time I have a curry at Charley Chans Chippy after a night out at the pub."

The mile walk home from the White Hart pub had helped to sober him up, but now the effects of the curry were beginning to make his digestive system rather uncomfortable. As usual Bert had forgotten his door key, and his wife Gwyneth would not be happy having to get out of bed to open the door to a drunken husband, especially as she was suffering with a very severe dose of flu. Banging a little louder on the door he raised his voice hoping that he wouldn't wake his neighbours

"Gwyneth, will you open this door and let me in?"

A light appeared in the upstairs bedroom, the window opened and barely able to speak Gwyneth asked, "Is that you, Bertram?"

Ever since they had first met she insisted on calling him Bertram and he found it embarrassing as he always preferred the name Bert. From an early age Gwyneth had enjoyed a privileged lifestyle, learning how to speak correctly and address people by their full name. She had worked for her father, a successful businessman who owned several factories. That was until his businesses collapsed, leaving him with huge debts. The family house was sold, which resulted in Gwyneth and her parents having to move into rented accommodation. The strain on her parents proved to be too much however, and in less than a year both had died. With no actual work skills or qualifications Gwyneth had no choice but to accept any employment available.

"No, it's the postman!" Bert replied sarcastically.

A moment's silence followed before Gwyneth answered: "Isn't it a little early for you to be delivering the mail, postman?"

Bert's bowels were now close to bursting. If she didn't open the door pretty quick and let him get to the toilet there would be an awful smell in the street and on Bert. Curbing the urge to express a few expletives whilst at the same time clenching the cheeks of his buttocks together, Bert replied:

"No dearest it is I, Bertram."

"Coming."

Seconds later Gwyneth opened the door, Bert gave her a quick kiss on the cheek and proceeded to make as quick an ascent as was humanly possible up the stairs. Gwyneth quickly closed the door and made her way up the stairs and back to her warm bed. Passing the bathroom door, she heard Bert exclaim, "Thank god!"

"Are you alright in there, why are you praying?"

"I am fine my dearest," Bert said, at the same time wafting his hand trying to disperse the smell even though the bathroom window was still closed. After raising himself from the toilet he flung open the bathroom window and began taking in deep breaths of air.

After all, Bert thought, there is only so much a man can take even if it was self-inflicted. Looking down at the toilet bowl, which after three flushes was still not in a suitable condition for Gwyneth to see, Bert wondered how he was going to clean it, because the toilet brush he had ordered from Andy Dickens, a local door-to-door salesman, had still not arrived.

"Oh I know, ideal substitute, problem solved," he said quietly.

Satisfied that everything was in order he washed his hands and went to bed. Tonight though, he would not be in the same bed as Gwyneth.

"Thank goodness it is Saturday," Bert said to himself as he awoke the next morning, while at the same time being careful not to raise the bed sheets too high as the smell from the previous night's curry still lingered.

Getting dressed, he made his way into the bathroom which still smelled from the previous night's near calamity. Even though he had left the bathroom window open the smell still lingered and so he decided to give the bathroom a generous spray with the air freshener. Gazing into the mirror as he slowly shaved he thought to himself, I'm not a bad looking bloke for my age, balding a little, slight beer belly, medium height, dark eyed. His dreamy thoughts suddenly returned to reality as his stomach reminded him that it was breakfast time. However, instead of his usual egg and bacon he decided that toast and jam was all he could eat. He had a quick look through the daily newspaper as he ate, afterwards deciding it was time to take a cup of tea up to Gwyneth and hoping she would be in a forgiving mood. He gave a gentle knock on the bedroom door before slowly opening it and stepping inside. The knock on the door was sufficient to wake her.

"Good morning dear. How are you feeling, any better?" he asked hesitantly, not quite knowing what response he would get.

Gwyneth gave a faint smile. "A little better dear, but I will stop in bed for a while longer," she replied.

Her smile gave Bert the confidence to approach the next subject.

"Don't forget it's the darts team presentation night at the White Hart pub tonight, and I would like you to be there as your bright-eyed and bushy-tailed self."

Gwyneth's smile briefly faded, but then she nodded her head in agreement, knowing that if she didn't go Bert would be disappointed as he always enjoyed her support.

"Well I must go dear, as I need to carry out the usual weekly maintenance on my van, you have a rest and I will see you later."

Bert smiled to himself as he went down the stairs. If Gwyneth came to the White Hart in the car he would be guaranteed a ride home because she never touched alcohol. He then decided to wash-up the few dishes in the sink before going to carry out the weekly maintenance on his van. Bert lived in the house where he was born in the village of Bentford. The house which had a large driveway was located in a quiet cul-de-sac. This driveway gave access to the rear of his house where an outbuilding served as a storage unit for his business. After leaving school he was employed by the postal service, eventually becoming a postman. But there was not enough challenge in delivering mail, and by sheer chance, after carrying out a few odd jobs for people in the village, he decided to go self-employed, doing anything which came his way from decorating to digging ditches. The death of his parents when he was twenty-five was a devastating blow, and he had lived alone until he met and married Gwyneth six years later.

Stepping outside into the garden he was greeted by the warmth of the sun on his face, which made him feel how good it was to be alive. He walked slowly down the garden path, at the same time peering through the ornamental bushes which divided his own garden from that of his neighbour Reg Armitage, who was usually out in his garden quite early. Reg was in his late sixties, a retired accountant who was very tall and thin with greying hair, and had a mostly pleasant attitude towards Bert. His wife Dolly however, seemed to live in a dream world. Very often she would go grocery shopping and come home without the groceries.

"Good morning Reg, are you alright then, lovely day?" Bert said cheerfully as he spotted Reg bending over his cold frame.

"Hello Bert," Reg replied without looking up at him.

Bert pondered briefly, as this was not the usual response from Reg who normally had a happy outlook on life.

"Something bothering you Reg, is the wife not feeling very well again?"

Reg turned around with a scowl on his face.

"Please, do not mention my wife."

"So sorry, didn't mean any offence," Bert said, taking a step back to create a space between them.

Reg's scowl briefly faded before it changed to an angry look: "Do you know what the stupid woman did yesterday?"

"No, but I am sure you are going to tell me," Bert replied

"She went for her regular appointment at the doctor's and the doctor diagnosed her as having an ulcerated colitis. But as usual her brain went into orbit and got all mixed up. She then phoned her mother and told her that she had an ulcerated clitoris!"

Reg's face had now turned bright red.

"The next I know her mother is phoning me demanding to know what I have been doing to her daughter!"

Reg turned his gaze back to Bert who by now was close to bursting with laughter, the corners of his mouth twitching as he tried to contain himself.

"Are you laughing at me?" Reg asked.

Bert could not answer, only shake his head.

"And do you know, she still asks for self-addictive stamps at the post office! Mrs Hopkins, the postmistress, says that when she retires from the post office she is going to write a book with my wife as the main character."

"Will this be a comedy?" Bert asked, trying to look serious.

The look on Reg's face was enough to tell Bert that it was time to leave, so taking a deep breath he managed to excuse himself and set off in the direction of his van, which was parked at the end of the driveway. He stopped briefly to admire his white van which had his name in large blue letters down either side, 'Richard B Head, Handyman Services'. Except for the odd scratch on it, the only other damage to it was where someone had scrawled the word 'Dick' above his name 'Head'. Opening the van door, he pulled the bonnet release catch and raised the bonnet. Taking a piece of tissue from his pocket he reached inside the engine compartment. Pulling out the engine oil dipstick it showed the oil level was down again.

"I definitely need to add some oil. Now how about that fan belt, the stupid thing is always making a funny noise," he muttered to himself.

Bert's hands were beginning to get quite black from the dirt around the engine. He was annoyed with himself for using a tissue instead of a piece of cloth. As he reached deeper into the engine compartment to check the fan belt tension, he tensed as a hand gently stroked down the cheek of his right buttock

"Reg, you dirty old man, I didn't think you cared for me. I will give you one second to stop!"

There was no answer and Bert tensed even more when seconds later another hand slid down his left buttock. Realising that there was someone there that he possibly didn't know, he quickly raised his head at the same time banging his head on the underside of the bonnet. Turning around to confront whoever it was, and with his hands raised to defend himself, he found himself face-to-face with Beryl.

"Hello Bert," she said smiling broadly, at the same time pressing herself closer to him, her low-cut white blouse showing off her large bust.

Beryl Harrison was a widow who had moved into the village five years earlier and from her first meeting with Bert she had shown a strong physical attraction to him. Bert was quite flattered at first as it gave his ego a lift, but he always tried to distance himself from her clutches. She never appeared to have any employment, but was quite content spending her time keeping her garden tidy and staying in contact with all of her neighbours, especially Bert who would duck out of her way if he saw her approaching. This time she had won. Beryl was in her mid to late thirties with a good figure, dark eyed, long black hair and at 5 feet 10 inches tall she was slightly taller than Bert.

"Hello Beryl," Bert stammered, as he let his hands slowly move away from the height of her chest until they were outstretched, like someone being held hostage in an armed robbery. The last thing he wanted was to put a greasy mark on her white blouse.

"Oh you poor thing, now you have bumped your head. Let me take a look."

Before Bert could move, she reached out with her left hand, pulled his head tight into her chest and began stroking the back of his head with her right hand.

"Please Beryl," Bert said in a barely audible voice because of his face being buried deep into her chest.

"Now that is what I like to hear you say, Bert."

Bert managed to turn his head slightly as he fought for breath.

"Please Beryl, no! If my wife shows up what do I say?"

"I will tell her that you were feeling faint and I offered to revive you using my chest-to-face revival technique."

She slightly eased her grip on Bert's head which gave him the opportunity to take a deep breath.

"And where did you learn to do that?" he asked.

"Oh I didn't learn it, you silly, I developed it through practice."

She once again pulled Bert's head closer into her chest and continued stroking the back of his head. By now, however, Bert had stopped worrying about Gwyneth showing up as the warmth of Beryl's chest was having a very comforting effect.

"Are you feeling any better now?" Beryl asked.

Bert managed to draw his head away from her.

"Yes," he replied giving a deep cough. "Thank you."

"Well, that has got to be the finest piece of stand and deliver I have ever seen! Can I be next?"

It was Reg, who had noticed Beryl as she had made her way down the driveway towards Bert.

"No you cannot Reggie. Bert is my little sweetie, aren't you?"

A red-faced Bert gave a half nod.

"If you stand like that for much longer, Bert, you will be able to hire yourself out as a scarecrow," Reg said as Bert stood breathing heavily with his arms outstretched.

"What were you two up to anyway? Does your Gwyneth know, Bert?" Reg said with a smile on his face.

Bert finally managed to speak.

"There is nothing happening between Beryl and I, and there is no need for my wife to know about Beryl reviving me when I had a fainting spell. Besides, she came to offer me something. I mean she had a job for me didn't you, Beryl?"

"Yes my sweet, can you come around to my place sometime? There is something I would like you to look at, but do make sure your hands are clean!"

She gently kissed Bert on his forehead, gave him a broad smile and walked away.

Reg closely studied Beryl's gently swaying hips as she walked away.

"You lucky devil, how do you manage it Bert? I would do cartwheels to have her chasing me!"

Bert had now recovered sufficiently from his embarrassment.

"Reg, she has had this thing for me ever since we met and she won't leave me alone. If Gwyneth ever found out she would crucify me!"

"Tell you what Bert, I bet Beryl could crucify you even better!"

Bert quickly changed the subject: "What did you want Reg?"

"Nothing much really, I just thought I would come down for a chat, after all I was a little bit sharp with you when we were talking about my wife earlier, thought I owed you an apology."

"No you don't owe me an apology Reg, we all have our odd moments, especially where women are concerned."

They continued talking for another half hour until Reg decided to carry on with his gardening, leaving Bert to complete the maintenance on his van. At 12.15 PM Bert decided to look in on Gwyneth. He slowly opened the bedroom door and stepped inside. Gwyneth was awake and reading a book.

"Are you feeling any better dear?" he asked.

Gwyneth gave him a weak smile: "Yes thank you dear, but my nose is still blocked up with this terrible catarrh and I can't smell a thing."

"So, you will be okay to give me a lift home from the pub tonight, after the darts presentation?"

Her smile faded for a second, and then she nodded.

"So if I set off walking to the pub about seven o'clock and you drive down for nine o'clock, you won't have to spend all night in a stuffy atmosphere."

Again she nodded, gave a sigh, placed her book on the bedside table, closed her eyes and went back to sleep.

Saturday Night

Although Bert enjoyed being free and able to spend time at the White Hart pub, he very often missed not having a family. They had tried to start a family, but it seemed Gwyneth was never able to get pregnant. He spent the rest of the afternoon reading the newspaper and watching the horse racing before falling asleep. When he awoke it was too late to begin cooking a dinner, and so he decided it would be quicker for him to have grilled fish fingers with a few slices of bread and butter. As he ate he couldn't stop his thoughts drifting back to his earlier encounter with Beryl. Wow what a woman!

After tidying up the kitchen and washing the dishes he took a shower. The smell from the toilet of the previous night's episode had finally disappeared. Checking to make sure the alarm clock was set for 8.00 PM, he placed it close to the bedroom where Gwyneth was sleeping. Got to make sure I have a lift home tonight, he thought to himself. Putting on his jacket, he set off on a steady stroll to the White Hart pub.

"This is the life - a lovely summers evening, a steady walk to the pub, a few pints of beer, what more could anyone wish for?" he said to himself

Bert often talked to himself when he was alone. Some people said to him that it was an early sign of madness. Twenty minutes later he arrived at the White Hart pub.

"Good evening Val, evening Ken," Bert said as he walked into the main bar of the White Hart pub. "I hope that you are both in good health."

Val and Ken Dixon had run the White Hart pub for the past eight years and were quite popular amongst everyone in the surrounding area.

"Can't complain, and if I did nobody would listen!" replied Ken as he filled a glass with beer for Bert.

The bar was quiet except for a few people who Bert did not recognise. Picking up his beer he took a sip from it to avoid any spillage and then made his way into the games room. The only person in the games room was Danny. He was dressed in a bright pink shirt decorated with flowers, white shorts and open-toed sandals.

"Hello Danny. What are you doing hiding away in here?" Bert asked

Danny was about the same age as Bert, and they had both attended the same village school. Danny was gay and many locals tended to give him the cold shoulder, but he and Bert had always remained good friends. Danny was leant with his left elbow on the bar, his right hand holding a half empty pint of lager. The sad look on his face told Bert that all was not well.

"Where is he then?" Bert asked

"Who are you asking about, Bert?" Danny replied.

"Your best mate, Phillip."

"Gone," Danny said in a sad tone of voice.

"Gone, gone where? Was he not very well? Not like him to leave early."

"He has gone, finished, we are not a couple any more. He left last week, so sad really."

Bert noticed a tear forming in the corner of Danny's eye.: "What happened then, I always thought you two were happy together?"

"We were, but the problem was the wind."

"What wind? It's been quite pleasant and sunny lately, you must get different weather down your end of the village." Bert said

"Not that kind of wind, the other, you know."

Easing himself from the bar and with his left hand he pointed downwards and towards his rear.

"Oh, that sort of wind!" Bert said. "Well most people get a bit of that now and again."

"Yes but his never stopped, it was constant. It got so bad that all of my friends began to call him chocolate lips! It was so embarrassing that I was forced to tell him he had to go, but I do miss him."

Bert placed a consoling hand on Danny's shoulder, giving it a gentle squeeze. Members of the darts team began to arrive, along with their friends and supporters who gradually began filling the games room. For the next hour Bert passed the time chatting with various team members and friends. He glanced at the clock at the bar which now showed 8.45 PM. Another fifteen minutes and Gwyneth should arrive.

"Harry."

Harry turned as he heard Bert call his name. Harry Patterson was the darts team captain, He was a short stocky figure with a rounded face and ruddy complexion which was due mainly to the amount of beer he consumed rather than the fresh country air as many people thought.

"Can you reserve a seat at your table for Gwyneth? She should be here in about fifteen minutes."

"No problem, Bert."

Ten minutes later the games room door opened and Gwyneth came in. Bert gave her a quick wave and she made her way towards him.

"Here you are dear, I have saved you a seat," Bert said as he helped her take off her coat.

"Now, what would you like to drink?"

"A lemonade will be fine, thank you Bertram."

Bert made his way over to the bar where Harry Patterson was ordering another drink.

"Pint of bitter and an orange juice please Ken, and excuse me for asking but do you have a problem with the drains in the pub as there seems to be a smell like sewage?" Harry asked.

Ken raised his head and sniffed.

"Never had a problem before, but now you mention it, Harry, there is a faint odour. I must phone the brewery and ask them to look into it," he replied.

Bert had also noticed a few people sniffing the air as if there was something not right.

"Yes Bert, your usual pint of bitter and a lemonade for Gwyneth?"

"Yes please, Ken."

Picking up his drinks, Bert made his way towards where Gwyneth was sitting. Danny, who had been talking with Gwyneth, stepped aside as Bert approached with the drinks. A hand on Bert's shoulder caused him to halt and turn his head.

"Hello Bert." It was Andy Dickens, the local salesman.

"Hello Andy, it has been a long time since you were in here. Can I speak to you a little later?"

Bert then turned to make his way back to Gwyneth.

"Bert, before you go, that toilet brush you ordered has arrived. Did you want to collect it or would you like me to deliver it?"

Bert stood motionless as the colour drained from his face.

"Oh my God, no," he said silently.

He lurched forward as if a hand had reached out and given him a push, sending his pint of beer over Gwyneth's head. Gwyneth's reaction was to jump up, resulting in the glass of lemonade Bert was holding in his other hand to cascade down the back of her dress. Everyone in the bar stopped and turned at the sound of Gwyneth's yell of distress.

Bert was the first to speak: "Danny, that was a silly thing you did, touching my rear end when I am carrying drinks. I know you are single once again but please keep your hands to yourself in future."

Danny stood motionless with his glass of beer halfway to his lips.

"I never touched..." he began to explain.

Before he could say any more Bert interrupted him: "There is no need to apologise, Danny, I know it was never your intention to cause me any offence."

He turned his attention back towards Gwyneth who had stood up and was now shaking her beer-soaked hair, looking more like a rain-soaked, long-haired dog than a human being. Several people in the games room began showing signs of laughter.

"Now please everyone, do not laugh, for as you can see my wife has had an unfortunate accident which I do not consider funny," Bert said in a serious tone of voice.

He then turned towards the bar: "Val, do you have a towel to assist my wife in getting dry?"

Val appeared from behind the bar with a towel in her hand. She pushed Bert aside.

"Get out of my way Bert, men are so stupid! Come with me Gwyneth, let me get you cleaned up in the back room."

"And when you are ready I will order you a taxi," Bert said.

"No you won't, I will drive her home and make sure she is safely tucked up in bed," Val replied.

Bert decided it was better to keep quiet.

"You crafty devil, Danny never touched you. Why did you want to get rid of your wife? Have you got a bit on the side?"

Turning around, Bert found himself facing Andy.

"No I do not have a bit on the side, and keep your voice down!"

Bert took Andy by the arm and guided him towards the furthest corner of the games room. Glancing around to make sure no one was listening, Bert proceeded to tell him

about his Friday night episode with the toilet.

"Anyway, after I flushed the toilet the toilet bowl was still not clean, and not having a toilet brush I used the next best thing - Gwyneth's hairbrush. And now it seems I didn't clean the hairbrush properly…"

At that point, Andy interrupted: "So what you are saying is, before Gwyneth came out tonight, she brushed her hair with the same brush that you used to clean the toilet?!"

Andy screwed up his face: "Bert, that is disgusting!"

"I know it is Andy, but keep it to yourself because if Gwyneth ever found out my life would not be worth living. And yes, it would be a good idea for you to deliver the toilet brush as soon as possible."

"So that will be drinks all round for the darts team, courtesy of Bert, for the remainder of the evening."

Turning around, Bert was confronted by Harry Patterson and two other members of the darts team who had overheard their conversation.

"Well, I…" Bert stammered as he struggled to find an excuse.

"No need to explain any more Bert, we will not say a word. Just hope you are feeling flush!"

With a huge sigh Bert accepted defeat, pulled out his wallet and ordered the drinks. After a few more pints his worries eased away, feeling even better when he was awarded the trophy for the most consistent highest darts scorer of the season. He left the pub just after midnight, heading for a long walk home.

"Good thing I remembered my door key," he said to himself.

On arriving home, the first thing he did was to throw Gwyneth's hairbrush in the dustbin.

Sunday Onwards, Tread Carefully

On Sunday morning Bert allowed himself some extra time in bed, getting up at 9 AM. Gwyneth was already up, sitting in the kitchen sipping a cup of tea.

"Good morning dear," Bert said brightly.

Gwyneth responded with a half-smile

"Good morning Bertram," she replied coldly. "Did you sleep well?"

"Yes, thank you. Did you dear?"

"No, I did not," she replied tersely.

Bert decided that this was a good time to say nothing, so pouring himself a cup of tea he excused himself and sat in the garden to enjoy the morning air. In another two hours or so Gwyneth would be in a much better mood. He had almost finished his tea when Gwyneth tapped him on the shoulder.

"Bertram, telephone."

He followed her into the kitchen and picked up the telephone. "Hello."

"Morning Bert, it's me Billy."

Billy Simons was Bert's labourer. He had worked for Bert for three years. Billy was not a well-educated individual, but at a little over six feet tall and of heavy build, Bert appreciated his physical ability whenever there was any heavy work to be done.

"Hello Billy. How are you? Are the family okay?"

"Yes thank you, Bert. Are you going to pick me up in the morning?"

"Yes Billy, 8 30 AM if that's okay."

"Thanks Bert, cheerio."

Bert put the phone down and went outside. The remainder of Sunday was very quiet in the Head household, with Gwyneth gradually forgetting about the previous night's episode. That night a smile crossed Bert's face as he snuggled up to her in bed.

Bert arrived outside Billy's caravan at 8.30 AM the following morning. Billy lived in a large static caravan on a two-acre plot of land owned by a local farmer. He had five children, the youngest being two years old. The door of the caravan opened and Billy came out, followed by his wife Doreen. She was a big buxom woman with a happy nature, which was a requirement when taking care of five children. She gave Bert a friendly wave.

"Good morning Bert, where are we off too today?" Billy asked as he climbed into the van.

"We are going to Mrs Pitswell's again. And if you have to speak to her, please try to remember her name is Mrs Pitswell, and not what you called her last time, Mrs Titswell!"

"Sorry Bert."

"It seems there is still a problem with the drains in that narrow passage at the rear of the cottage, and so it will mean more digging."

"And try to remember not to mention anything about back passages, like the last time you asked if she still had a problem with her back passage!"

"Yes Bert."

Mrs Pitswell lived ten miles away in an old cottage which had a large walled garden. Arriving at the cottage, Mrs Pitswell was already outside spraying the rose bushes with insecticide.

"Good morning Mrs Pitswell," Bert said.

"Good morning Mr Head," she replied at the same time giving Billy an icy stare.

She was a widow in her late sixties, but very independent and active.

"I understand from the engineer's report that there is still a problem with the drains down the back passage," Bert said.

She tensed slightly at this comment.

"Yes that is correct, Mr Head," she replied.

Billy began unloading the van while Bert went down the passage which divided the cottage and an old workshop, and began to remove the covers which concealed the trench which they had dug previously. Bert volunteered to do the digging for the first hour or so while Billy wheeled away the soil, which he tipped into a corner of the walled garden. Bert was bending over in the trench trying to remove an extra-large stone, when he was interrupted by Mrs Pitswell.

"Mr Head, I have observed your man from my kitchen window doing a most unusual act. Is he an amateur ballet dancer?"

"Let me take a look, Mrs Pitswell," Bert said, climbing out of the trench and making his way into the garden.

Billy was standing with his back towards Bert, his right hand on the wall, his left leg on the heap of soil in the wheelbarrow. Every few seconds he would raise his leg from the soil and give it a quick shake. Bert made his way towards Billy.

"Billy what are you doing, are you alright?" he asked quietly.

A look of embarrassment crossed Billy's face.

"Yes I am okay, Bert, but it's my scrotum that's the problem."

"Have you hurt it?"

"No it is stuck to my leg and I am trying to shake it free."

"Why not use your hand?"

"Can't do that because my hands are covered in soil."

"You do realise that Mrs Pitswell has been watching your performance."

Billy immediately stood upright slightly red faced.

"Sorry, Bert."

"Anyway, get the barrow emptied and pretty soon it will be time for our lunch break."

Thirty minutes later they stopped for lunch, deciding to sit outside and make the most of the good weather. Billy bit into his sandwich which made a loud crunching sound.

"Billy, what have you got in your sandwiches, gravel?" Bert asked.

"No, Coco Pops," Billy replied.

"Coco Pop sandwiches! Whose idea was that?"

"Mine," Billy said proudly. "Bert, can I ask you something?"

"It depends on what you want to ask."

"How come your Gwyneth talks posh?"

"The simple answer to that it's because she is from aristocracy."

"Where's that then?"

"Where's what?"

"That ari-aristocracy place," Billy asked.

"Aristocracy is not a place; it means someone who comes from a higher social class, people who have titles and things like that."

"Why did she marry you then, was she desperate?"

Bert sighed. There were times when Billy got under his skin with some of his questions.

"No, she was not desperate, her father was a businessman who went bankrupt and I met Gwyneth in London, in Soho."

A worried look crossed Billy's face.

"In Soho, London. You mean she was doing it, selling her body to make a living because her dad had got no money."

"No she was not doing it, she was working in a restaurant and I went in for a meal and that's how we met."

"What were you doing in Soho, Bert?"

Bert rolled his eyes, finished drinking his tea and stood up.

"Back to work Billy, more digging to do."

The rest of the afternoon passed quickly as they continued digging out the trench. At 4.30 PM Bert decided it was time to finish work for the day. It took only a few minutes to load up the van and set off for home.

"Billy, that bloke in the pub on Friday night, the one who said your wife was ugly, why didn't you offer to take him outside and punch him?"

"Well she is ugly, and I always admire someone for being honest. That's another reason why I married her, less chance of her running off with someone else."

Bert shook his head in disbelief.

"How many years have you been married, Billy?"

"Ten years next month. We first met on a pig farm. Those were the days, listening to the sound of little trotters, the grunting and the smells."

A look of dreamy bliss was etched on Billy's face as they stopped at Billy's caravan.

"See you in the morning, Billy."

"Okay, Bert."

Gwyneth had Bert's supper cooked and ready for the table. Bert changed out of his work clothes, washed his hands and sat down at the table. The aroma of Gwyneth's cooking told Bert what he would be having for his supper today, one of his favourite meals, a meat and potato pie. Although she had enjoyed a privileged lifestyle Gwyneth was a very good cook.

After eating his supper, Bert spent a few minutes scanning through the news in the local newspaper, while Gwyneth studied the minutes of the recent meeting of the WI of which she was the secretary. When Bert came downstairs from taking a shower, Gwyneth was sat outside on the garden seat enjoying the evening sun.

"Oh by the way Bertram, you had a phone call today from Beryl. You know, the widow, the one who always speaks highly of you."

"She said can you go around one day soon as possible, because she would like something fixing."

Bert turned away from Gwyneth as he began to blush.

"And I can guess what that is," Bert muttered under his breath.

"What did you say dear?"

"Nothing dearest, just talking to myself," Bert replied.

Tuesday Blues

The next morning, Bert arrived at his usual time of 8.30 AM at Billy's caravan. Billy came out a few minutes later and kissed his wife Doreen goodbye. He climbed into the van, muttered good morning to Bert, put on his seatbelt and slumped into the corner of his seat with a very sad look on his face.

"And a very good morning to you," Bert said. "Did you get out of the wrong side of the bed this morning, or was your porridge cold?"

"You wouldn't be interested in my problems," Billy replied.

"Try me, maybe I can help. Are you short of money?"

"No, it's the wife. She's pregnant again."

"Again! And how did that…" Bert decided not to proceed with that question, because Billy would probably want to go into all the fine details.

"How many will this be?"

"Six."

"Six! You always said that you didn't want any more. Don't you ever take precautions?"

"Well we always make sure the kids are asleep."

"I didn't mean that sort of thing. I meant some sort of protection to stop her getting pregnant."

"Well a friend of Doreen's suggested that we should try the rhythm method, but when she told me, I said I didn't want a radio in the bedroom. And another thing, how do you know what sort of music to tune into?"

Bert looked straight ahead to stop himself laughing.

"Look Billy, the only sure way to stop your wife getting pregnant is for you to have the snip."

A look of horror crossed Billy's face: "You mean castration."

"No, not castration."

"It is an operation called a vasectomy which takes about fifteen minutes. What the doctor does is give you a local anaesthetic down there," Bert said pointing down at Billy's groin. "He then snips the tubes that carry the sperm, and hey presto no more kids!"

"But won't my testicles drop off?"

"No, they won't drop off."

A minor look of relief crossed Billy's face.

"Bert, how is it you and Gwyneth never had any kids?"

"I suppose we were never lucky," Bert replied.

"No, it doesn't come down to luck, Bert. What you have to do…" Billy said.

"Billy, I know what to do. Personally I think it was possibly my sperm was no good. I've never had any tests done on it, but some clever wag in the pub suggested that it might just be good enough for making meringue!"

A puzzled look appeared on Billy's face.

"Would you need to add sugar to it to make it taste good?"

"To make what taste good?"

"The meringue," Billy said.

Frustration showed on Bert's face: "He was joking when he said that Billy!"

Billy nodded as if he understood but Bert knew that he would be pondering on that for much of the day. They arrived at Mrs Pitswell's to begin another day of digging as the engineers had still not found the problem with the drains. Mrs Pitswell was not home as she visited her sister Betty every Tuesday who lived over 20 miles away. The rest of the day was incident free, except for Billy falling down the trench when he attempted to lean against the wall without realising he was standing on the wrong side of the trench.

At 4.30 PM Bert decided to finish work. They loaded up the van and set off for home. After driving a short distance Bert's nose began to twitch.

"Smells like someone is spreading manure," he said to Billy.

A look of embarrassment spread across Billy's face.

"No it isn't manure, Bert, it's me," Billy said.

"You, what do you mean it's you? When did you last have a shower?"

"About a week ago. It's my contribution to save the planet from disaster."

"Save it from disaster, if you carry on like this you will gas everyone on it! What does your wife say about you smelling like that?"

"Nothing, because she smells just the same, she hasn't showered either."

"And what about the kids?" Bert asked.

"They have been banned from school until they have had a wash."

"Anyhow, might I suggest that you have a shower tonight and if the planet collapses tomorrow it will be your fault for being clean."

"Yes Bert."

Bert dropped Billy off and continued home. He hadn't yet decided what work he would be doing tomorrow even though he had a full list of jobs available. He also knew that many of his customers accepted that he could arrive at a moment's notice. Perhaps he might even go to the builder's merchant and pick up some materials.

"Hello dear, have you had a good day?" Bert asked, as he walked into the kitchen where Gwyneth was busy preparing a meal.

"To be quite honest, Bertram, I have not been feeling very well, just a little queasy now and then. Beryl phoned again, asking that you go round to try and sort out that work you did for her last month."

"Yes okay, I will do that tomorrow, although I did tell her it was only a temporary repair anyway."

"This time I will take Billy with me", Bert muttered to himself. On his last visit he was lucky to escape in one piece, although he did enjoy the attention.

"Gwyneth, if you aren't feeling any better tomorrow I think you should consider making an appointment to see the doctor," Bert said

"Yes I will do that, now sit down and have your supper."

"Thank you dear."

After his supper Bert spent the rest of the evening pottering about in the garden until it was dark.

Wednesday

He picked Billy up the next morning.

"Where are we off to today, Bert?"

"First of all we are going to the builder's merchant to pick up a few supplies, and then we have to complete a temporary job that I did for Beryl Harrison."

"Is that the same Beryl who lives near you Bert, the one with the big chest? She likes you Bert."

"The very same, and yes she does like me."

They collected the few supplies that Bert needed and set off for Beryl's house. She answered Bert's knock on the door but her smile faded slightly when she saw Billy.

"Come in, Bert. I think the bathroom should be tidy but first of all let me take a look. Follow me!"

Bert, with Billy close behind, followed her up the staircase, hardly taking his eyes off her swaying hips. She went into the bathroom and quickly closed the door after Bert had got inside, which prevented Billy from entering. A look of panic spread across Bert's face.

"Oh I just remembered, I need to turn the water off at the stopcock in the kitchen," Bert said.

Beryl stepped between Bert and the bathroom door.

"Billy," Beryl called out. "Can you go down into the kitchen and turn the water off at the stopcock? You will find it under the kitchen sink."

"Okay," Billy replied.

"Now Bert, how is your head?"

Before Bert could move, she reached out and pulled his head close into her chest, at the same time pressing herself against him.

"I have missed you Bert, you are so lovely," she whispered to him.

"Oh please, Beryl," Bert said as he struggled for breath. "Please."

"I love it when you say please, and you said it twice this time!"

Relaxing her grip on his head she pressed her lips onto Bert's, her arms firmly pinning his to his side. The sound of Billy's

135

footsteps reaching the top of the stairs caused her to ease her grip on Bert.

"Waters off," said Billy.

She drew back her lips from Bert's, gave him a lingering smile, opened the bathroom door and went downstairs, leaving him all red faced. Billy poked his head around the door.

"You alright Bert, you look a little bit flushed?"

"Yes I am, now could you go down to the van and get my tool bag and the new fittings for the bath drain."

"Okay Bert."

After installing the new bath drain fittings, they tidied up and went downstairs. Beryl was waiting at the bottom of the stairs.

"All finished now Beryl. I will mail you my bill in a few days."

"I would much prefer it if you brought it in person as the personal touch is so much better," she replied, at the same time giving him a lingering smile.

Bert didn't respond to her suggestion, but very politely said his goodbye and followed Billy out to the van. One of these days, he thought to himself, one of these days.

Climbing into the van, Bert decided that as it was nearly lunchtime and being so close to his house, he decided that Billy could have lunch with himself and Gwyneth.

"Hello dear," Bert said as he walked into the kitchen.

"Hello, Bertram. Hello, Billy. I will boil some water and make you both a cup of tea."

"Hello, Mrs Head," Billy replied, knowing that she always appreciated being formally addressed.

Billy stood on one leg, leaning against the kitchen door frame as he removed one of his work boots. Upon removing the boot, he transferred his weight to the other leg with the intention of trying to lean against the door frame, however, as he had forgotten to turn around there was nothing to lean against, which resulted in him falling over. Before Bert could catch him Billy had fallen outside onto the patio. Billy picked himself up, having totally destroyed an apple tree which had stood in a large plant pot just outside the door which Bert had been hoping to transplant the following year.

"Are you alright?" Bert asked as he helped Billy back to his feet.

"Yes thanks, it's a good thing you had that big plant pot there for me to fall on or I could have really hurt myself."

"Yes, it certainly is your lucky day," Bert replied, at the same time gazing sadly at the broken tree.

Gwyneth came outside and taking Billy by the arm guided him into the kitchen and sat him down at the table.

"Now you sit down there Billy whilst I get you a nice cup of tea. Bertram, open a tin of soup for this poor injured man, we can't allow him to eat sandwiches after such a terrible accident."

"Yes dearest."

"Oh by the way Bertram, I have an appointment at the doctor's surgery tomorrow morning."

"Yes I think that is a good idea if you are still not feeling very good," Bert replied.

After eating his lunch, Bert settled down to read the newspaper while Billy went outside and tried to repot Bert's apple tree. Thirty minutes later Bert put down his newspaper: "Must be off now, Gwyneth," he said, at the same time giving her a kiss.

"Yes dear, be careful. See you later."

Billy was waiting outside.

"Where are we off to now, Bert?"

"The first call is to a Mr Atkinson who lives down Oak Lane. He wants an estimate for rebuilding a wall. Hopefully we could get some extra work there as I am informed that he is doing a few alterations inside the house."

A look of anguish crossed Billy's face: "Did you say Mr Atkinson who lives down Oak Lane?"

"Yes, why is that a problem?"

"I don't like it down there, it's spooky. When we were kids that Mr Atkinson caught me and my brother pinching apples from his orchard and he locked us up all afternoon in his shed."

"Well that was your fault for pinching his apples. Would you like it if he came to your place and pinched apples from your tree?"

"But we didn't have an apple tree, that's why we were pinching his!"

Bert shook his head and concentrated on his driving. He drove slowly down Oak Lane. Although he was familiar with Oak Lane he had never bothered trying to remember any of the house names.

"Here we are - Meadow Cottage," Bert said, turning the van into the driveway of a house which stood behind some large oak trees.

Bert stopped the van in the front of the house, which certainly looked in need of some renovation work. At first glance the structure of the house looked quite good, the window frames however, had begun to rot and the wall surrounding the garden had partially fallen over. The garden, which had been badly neglected, was now overgrown with weeds and long grass. Bert climbed out of the van while Billy remained in his seat with an anxious look on his face.

"It's no good sitting there looking all scared, Billy, I need you to hold the measuring tape," Bert said as he studied the area around the house.

Billy climbed out of the van at the same time nervously glancing around. He hurried over to where Bert was standing.

"Bert, can we hurry up and get out of here? I'm frightened, I don't want to meet that Mr Atkinson again."

"Well the sooner we get this wall measured up the sooner we can leave, you great big chicken!"

"It's alright for you, Bert, you don't know what he is like," Billy replied as he took the end of the tape measure.

"Can I help you gentlemen?" said a voice from behind them.

Billy reacted by releasing the end of the tape measure which snapped back into its holder, trapping Bert's finger. Turning around, Bert found himself facing an elderly man who stood approximately five foot six inches in height. And in Bert's estimation he looked to be about seventy-five years of age.

"Mr Atkinson?" Bert asked.

The old man nodded. Bert held out his hand and introduced himself.

"Bert Head, you phoned and asked me to give you an estimate for rebuilding a wall."

The old man shook Bert's hand.: "Oh yes, so good of you to come. Some people are so unreliable these days."

He stepped to his right to get a better look at Billy who was standing behind Bert, still with a nervous look on his face.

"And this, I trust, is your helper."

"Yes, this is Billy, Billy Simons, an excellent worker, one of the best," Bert replied.

Billy nervously held out his hand towards the old man. The old man shook Billy's hand at the same time giving him a closer look.

"Haven't we met before? I'm sure I know you from somewhere, never forget a face."

Bert quickly changed the subject.: "Is it just this wall which you want rebuilding Mr Atkinson?" Bert asked pointing to the garden wall.

"Andy," said the old man. "Call me, Andy. I much prefer an informal approach."

Bert nodded in agreement.

"For the moment yes, but later on I may require you to carry out more work for me, if that would be convenient. As you can see, the house is in a bit of a sorry state. About ten years ago my dear wife died, I had a nervous breakdown and I let the house get into disrepair but now I have decided to restore it to its former glory."

"Now I must be going, some very important business to attend to," he continued. 'I will leave you two gentlemen to carry on with your measuring. And please, don't bother with estimates for the building work, if you can just order the materials and complete the work. Money is no object. You have an honest face, Mr Head."

As he walked away he glanced back at Billy, obviously trying to remember where he had seen him before. Minutes later, they heard the sound of an engine start up and a large Mercedes car appeared from the other side of the house and headed off up the driveway. Bert turned around to face Billy who was stood behind him still with a nervous look on his face.

A broad smile crossed Bert's face: "And you were frightened of him."

"But we were only kids, and he had a big stick!"

After they had measured up the wall Bert decided it was time to take Billy home. Arriving back at his own home Bert was greeted by the rich aroma of his evening meal. After they had eaten, Bert helped Gwyneth with washing the dishes. He then settled down to estimate the materials needed for Mr Atkinson's wall.

Thursday

The sun was shining brightly the following morning when Bert arrived to collect Billy.

"Good morning, Billy. How are you this lovely sunny day?" Bert asked as Billy climbed into the van.

"Okay, I suppose," Billy replied, a bleary-eyed look on his face.

"The kids keeping you busy?"

Billy nodded and sighed: "They drive me mad, but I still love them."

"So you should. Sometimes I envy you Billy, not having any kids of my own."

"You can borrow mine for the weekend if you feel lonely!"

Bert didn't reply.

"Where are we off to today, Bert?"

"We are going to Mr Atkinson's to begin demolishing the garden wall and I have arranged for a rubbish skip to be delivered later this morning."

A brief look of fright crossed Billy's face.

"Don't worry, Billy, I will protect you if he brings out his big stick!"

When they arrived at Meadow Cottage Mr Atkinson was walking in the overgrown garden probing through the grass with a broom handle.

"Bert, he's got a stick. He must have recognised me!"

"Well, I think if you promised to buy him two pounds of apples he would probably forgive you."

A puzzled look appeared on Billy's face as he tried to figure out whether Bert was serious or not.

"Good morning Andy, it's a lovely day again," Bert said, as he opened the van door.

"Yes, it certainly is," he replied at the same time staring at Billy, who with a nervous, tense look on his face slowly climbed out of the van.

"I'm sure we have met before," he said staring at Billy.

He disappeared into the house, leaving them to begin the task of demolishing the rest of the wall. The rubbish skip arrived later that morning, and by four-thirty that afternoon half of the wall had been loaded into it.

After supper that evening, Bert concentrated on bringing his accounts up to date and preparing the bills for his customers, at the same time agonising over the one for Beryl, still being undecided as to whether he should deliver it in person or post it. A tap on his shoulder brought him quickly back to reality.

"Bertram, that lovely lady Beryl called here today and said that, although you are probably very busy, could you spare any time to give her an estimate on doing some decorating for her. She said it was in a bedroom."

Friday

Bert took a deep breath as he knocked on Beryl's door the following morning. He had decided to take Billy with him as a possible safeguard against Beryl's advances, but he knew that one day she would ensnare him. His thoughts drifted at the possible outcome. These thoughts stopped abruptly as Beryl opened the door. She was dressed in a pale blue housecoat which reached down to just above her ankles. It was fastened at the waist by a matching belt, allowing it to hang loosely on her body.

"Hello, Bert. Come in."

Her smile which had initially greeted Bert faded slightly as she saw Billy. The movement of her stepping aside revealed to Bert that she was wearing very little beneath her housecoat. Bert stepped into the hallway, followed by Billy.

"Now Bert, have you brought your tape measure?"

"Yes," Bert replied.

"What I require is a bedroom to be completely redecorated. I have already decided on the style of wallpaper, so if you can measure the bedroom and let me know how many rolls I would need to buy, that would be wonderful."

Her smile had returned to its full glow as she stood up close to Bert, her perfume although not overpowering was enough to give Bert desirable thoughts, even more so now she had allowed her housecoat top to drop open.

"Which bedroom is it Beryl?" Bert stammered as he desperately tried to avert his gaze away from her chest.

"If you come with me I will show you."

"Now Billy, if you can wait here in the hallway, I can assist Bert by holding the end of the tape measure."

Bert began to open his mouth as if to protest, but she reached out and gently placed her finger on his lips, at the same time giving him a quiet shush.

"Come along, Bert," she said as she made her way towards the stairs.

His thoughts raced wildly as he followed the swaying taunting movement of her body up the stairs towards the bedroom. Taking a deep breath, he followed her into the bedroom. As Bert stepped inside the bedroom his fascination of Beryl's beauty switched off for a brief second as he cast his gaze around the room. His brief concentration was broken by the click of the bedroom door closing, but not before he had seen the large bed covered in fresh white sheets. Beryl had allowed Bert to move slightly in front of her, and now, as she closed the door, he turned to find that she had slipped off her housecoat, revealing her naked body.

His brain was in turmoil as he had never been unfaithful to Gwyneth in all their years of marriage. But here was a woman desperate for love and Bert's faith towards Gwyneth finally collapsed. He stood open-mouthed for a few seconds before his desire took over. He responded to her as she kissed him, clasping her and pinning her against the bedroom wall, the coldness of it making her gasp. He eased his grip on her as she began to unbutton his shirt, their lips still pressed together.

"Bert, can you get down here pretty quick? I think someone has just run into your van," Billy shouted.

Billy's shout brought a sudden end to their liaison. Their heavy breathing stopped as suddenly as it had begun. As their lips parted Bert called out in a very weak voice:

"Okay Billy."

"What did you say?"

Clearing his throat Bert responded a little louder: "Be there in a minute, Billy."

Bert began buttoning up his shirt as Beryl put on her housecoat. As he finished buttoning his shirt she reached forward and kissed him again. Opening the bedroom door, she made her way down the stairs, once again using that swaying taunting movement of her body which so tormented Bert.

Billy was already outside when Bert went out to see for himself what the commotion was all about. A cyclist lay in the road in a semi-conscious condition. His bicycle, with a buckled front wheel, was at the rear of Bert's van. A few people stood around him, one of whom was busy staunching the flow of blood from a deep cut on his leg. Within a few minutes an ambulance arrived, closely followed by a police car. The taking of statements took up the next hour. As Bert made his way back to Beryl's door, he was pleased that the cyclist didn't appear to be suffering any life-threatening injuries.

"Did you get the bedroom measurements, Bert?" Billy asked.

"No we didn't have time, Billy. Can you come and hold the tape measure for me?"

Bert and Beryl exchanged smiles as he and Billy made their way up the stairs. Fifteen minutes later Bert had completed taking the bedroom measurements. He and Billy made their way into the kitchen where Beryl was sat sipping a cup of tea.

"Would you both like a cup of tea?" she asked.

She motioned for Billy to sit on a chair at the end of the table, while she placed her chair close to where Bert had sat down. After she had poured out the two cups of tea she leaned across the table and passed one to Billy, as she did so her housecoat top dropped open revealing her naked breasts.

"Milk and sugar, Bert?" she asked.

"Yes please, just one," he replied.

She sat down close to Bert, rubbing her thigh up close to his. Bert took a deep breath as he tried to concentrate on estimating how much wallpaper would be required for the bedroom, at the same time feeling the warmth of Beryl's thigh gradually creeping through his jeans. Twice he came up with a figure and twice he scribbled it out as the warmth of her thigh pressing ever harder broke his concentration. Billy seemed to be in awe of Beryl, sitting staring at her, totally captivated by her beauty and the previous display of her breasts. He suddenly broke the silence as he became aware of Beryl looking at him and where his gaze was directed.

"Have you worked out the measurements, Bert?" he asked.

Bert had begun the calculations again, at the same time trying to keep his inner emotions under control as the nearness of Beryl made him ready to explode.

"Yes I have, Billy."

"Beryl, I think ten rolls of wallpaper will be sufficient, so if you let me know when you've bought them, I can give you a date when I can get started."

"Would you like me to come around in person to tell you?" she asked.

"No, just a phone call will be okay," Bert replied.

Drinking the remainder of his tea he stood up and made his way towards the door. Beryl followed close behind him with Billy taking up the rear. She opened the door then motioned for Billy to leave first. As Bert followed him her hand dropped down and caressed his right buttock.

"See you soon, Bert," she whispered.

"Yes, see you soon," he replied.

Once inside the van Bert gave a huge sigh of relief.

"I reckon she really likes you, Bert," Billy said. "And did you notice that she didn't have any clothes on underneath her housecoat? Wow what a view!"

"Yes I did notice, and please don't mention anything to Gwyneth about what you saw, she might get the wrong idea."

"Yes Bert."

They spent the rest of the day down Oak Lane at Meadow Cottage. Much to Billy's relief Mr Atkinson was away.

Saturday and Sunday were supposed to be for relaxing time in the Head household, but Gwyneth was still feeling unwell and a little queasy. This worried Bert, but not half as much as the prospect of his next meeting with Beryl. Bert did receive some good news on Saturday. A phone call from Mrs Pitswell informed him that the engineers had found the problem with the drains and it would be rectified in a few days, after which Bert could fill in the trench and complete the job. And to avoid any further close encounters with Beryl, Bert decided on the Sunday morning to walk down to the post box and post her the bill for the repairs to the bath.

Billy's Big Decision

On Monday morning Bert decided to call at the local grocery shop in the village for a few apples and oranges before picking up Billy. His neighbour Reg Armitage was in the shop as Bert walked in.

"Good morning, Bert."

"Good morning, Reg," Bert replied. "How are things in the Armitage household this bright and cheerful morning?"

"Oh, daft as ever," Reg sighed. "As you know Dolly goes to the pensioners keep fit in the village hall once a week. Well her friend Barbara has a husband, John who was recently diagnosed with tinnitus. Of course Barbara tells Dolly about John's condition. Dolly then gets it all mixed up, and is now telling everyone in the village that John has been diagnosed with 'tittinus!'"

Reg shook his head in despair, paid for his newspaper and left.

Billy was waiting as Bert drew up in the van.

"Good morning. Billy. Not a bad day, the birds are singing, nice to be alive."

"I suppose it is," Billy said glumly as he climbed into the van.

"And what has bitten you on the bum this morning, Mr Happiness?" Bert asked.

"I've done it," Billy replied. "I've taken your advice, made an appointment, and I am frightened."

"Frightened of what? And what advice did I give you to make you frightened?" Bert asked.

"Well, you know, that snip thing Bert," Billy replied as he nervously rubbed his hand across his face. "The doctor says that he can do the operation in about two weeks' time."

A smile spread across Bert's face: "Billy I am proud of you. You are a very brave man to make such a huge decision as that, and if they do drop off ask the doctor to sew them back on!"

The brief look of horror on Billy's face soon changed as Bert began laughing. They spent the rest of the day at Meadow Cottage, Oak Lane, tidying up the site in preparation for rebuilding the garden wall. The bricks, sand and cement arrived later that afternoon.

The remainder of the week soon passed, rebuilding the wall at Meadow Cottage and filling in the trench at Mrs Pitswell's. It was a quiet weekend for Bert and Gwyneth. He had his usual Saturday night visit to the White Hart pub, this time making sure to avoid any mishaps.

Another Monday morning, and Bert was preparing to leave home to pick up Billy at the usual time when Gwyneth called him back into the house. She handed him the telephone.

"Bertram, it's Billy, it sounds rather urgent."

"Hello Billy, is there a problem, are you not feeling very well?"

A nervous sounding Billy answered: "Bert, I have just had a phone call from the doctor's surgery to tell me that they have had a cancellation for tomorrow, and they can carry out my vasectomy operation in the morning at 10.15 AM."

"They also said that I must take at least a week off work after I have had the operation," he continued. "One other thing Bert, the receptionist at the surgery said that I must have a shave, does that mean I have to wear a collar and tie?"

"No, Billy. It means you must shave where they are going to make the incision, you know down below, and whatever you do don't use a cut-throat razor. Billy, I was joking about the cut-throat razor. And do not worry about having a week off work or even longer, I will still pay you your full wage."

A moments silence followed before Billy replied: "Thanks Bert, that's really great. Speak to you later, bye."

Not having a full calendar of work for the next two weeks Bert decided to call in and see Mr Atkinson at Meadow Cottage.

"I was just about to phone you, Bert," he said as Bert stepped out of his van. "I must say that you did an excellent job on the garden wall. Now you must let me know as soon as possible what I owe you. If you are still available would you be interested in replacing all the windows in the house?"

Bert didn't hesitate to say yes.

"And," continued Mr Atkinson, "when that is complete, you can renovate the whole of the house interior at your own pace."

Bert spent the remainder of the morning measuring up the windows in Meadow Cottage. Estimating the possible time and cost of the materials required to renovate the interior of Meadow Cottage took Bert the remainder of the afternoon. Although he felt apprehensive about going to Beryl's house to begin the decorating, perhaps now would be the perfect time, now that Billy was going to be incapacitated for at least a week. Although he still had nagging doubts about cheating on Gwyneth, his physical emotions stirred as he made his decision. That evening, while Gwyneth was taking a shower, he picked up the telephone and dialled Beryl's number.

At the breakfast table the next morning, Bert gazed thoughtfully at his toast as he took another sip of his tea. His mind was fixed firmly on Beryl and what lay ahead. He was suddenly jolted out of his thoughts by Gwyneth.

"Bertram, I forgot to mention it to you but I have an appointment at the doctor's surgery this morning at 9.30 AM. Where will you be working today?"

"Oh yes, dear. I have decided that I will go around to Beryl Harrison's this morning and begin stripping in the bedroom. Sorry! Stripping the bedroom wallpaper."

"That is a very good idea, Bertram, and no doubt she will enjoy the company. She must get terribly lonely being in that house all by herself."

Not for much longer, thought Bert to himself.

It was shortly after 9.30 AM when he arrived at Beryl's house. She must have been looking out for his arrival, for as he reached out to ring the doorbell the door opened and she beckoned him inside. The scent of her delicate perfume instantly aroused his emotions, but as he reached out to embrace her she gently pushed him away.

"Not here," she whispered. "Follow me."

Bert followed her as she began a slow ascent of the staircase, again taunted by the swaying of her hips hidden beneath her housecoat. Once inside the bedroom she ushered him towards the bed which was covered in a fresh white sheet. Bert gazed in awe as she let her housecoat slip off her shoulders revealing her semi naked body, her breasts supported by an uplifting bra which made them look even larger. His eyes slowly drifted down her body and onto the tiniest panties he had ever seen. Pushing him backwards onto the bed, she leaned over him and began to unbutton his sweat-soaked shirt. Bending her head closer she proceeded to kiss his now exposed torso, feeling his throbbing heart through her lips. Bert had now reached the point of bodily explosion. Raising herself upright Beryl reached to unhook her bra.

A heavy knocking on the house front door brought a sudden end to the proceedings. They both stared at each other in disbelief. Whoever it was, thought Bert, please go away. Here we are at the point of quenching our passion for each other and someone comes knocking on the door. Neither of them moved or spoke, afraid that whoever it was at the door might detect signs of occupancy.

A second bout of heavy knocking was followed by a loud voice: "Are you there Bert, it's me Billy?"

Bert shot upright and leapt off the bed, and with trembling fingers fastened his shirt. Shuffling across to the window he drew back the edge of the curtain and gave Billy a wave of acknowledgement. A broad smile crossed Billy's face, needless to say Bert did not respond in kind. He then turned to face Beryl, who in the final moments of her long-running desire for Bert, looked a picture of total sadness. As she put on her housecoat he drew her gently towards him and gave her a long lingering kiss. Then easing his hold on her he allowed his hands to slowly stroke down and over her hips.

"Next time, Beryl, next time," he whispered.

Her eyes lit up and a smile crossed her face.

"I will kill that, Billy," Bert muttered under his breath.

Giving Beryl the opportunity to get dressed, Bert went down and opened the door to let Billy into the house.

"Good morning, Bert. Guess what, my operation was cancelled at the last moment! I had just finished having my shave when the phone rang and it was the doctor's receptionist who said they couldn't do it today as the doctor had been called out on an emergency."

"And how did you know I was here at Beryl's?" Bert asked.

"Well I knew you wouldn't be at home and your mobile phone was switched off, so I phoned Gwyneth on her mobile phone and she told me you were here. My landlord, Mr Vickers, was on his way into the village and gave me a lift. Certainly gave you a surprise, Bert."

"Absolute knockout," Bert replied.

"You must have been busy upstairs, Bert. I was ringing the doorbell for nearly five minutes. I thought to myself, Bert must be busy stripping in the bedroom."

"Yes Billy, I was within touching distance of completing something which had been on my agenda for a long time!"

"And no doubt the opportunity will arise again," Billy replied.

Throughout the remainder of the day as they stripped the bedroom wallpaper, Bert couldn't help the occasional gaze at the bed and visualising what might have been. That evening Gwyneth informed him that her doctor was still unable to diagnose her medical condition, and that he had arranged another appointment for her on the Friday afternoon.

The decorating of Beryl's bedroom was completed by early Friday afternoon, and the only close contact she managed with Bert was when she insisted that he and Billy have their lunch break with her. This once again gave her the opportunity to sit up close to Bert and press her thigh against his.

Arriving home that Friday evening Bert parked his van in its usual place at the rear of his house. Ensuring that it was securely locked he walked towards the house, at the same time trying to guess what Gwyneth might have prepared for his supper. As he reached the house, the door was opened by Gwyneth who flung her arms around him, hugging him so tight that he could barely breathe. The smile which lit up her face told him that something special must have occurred.

"Bertram, you will never guess, it's happened!"

"What's happened? Have we won the lottery?"

"No, not the lottery. I am pregnant, the doctor confirmed it today!"

Bert's mouth dropped open and barely able to contain his delight he broke free from her hug and looked directly into her eyes.

"You are certain?"

"Yes!"

His thoughts raced wildly. After all these years of being told that he would never be a father, it had finally happened.

"But Gwyneth, we were told many years ago that it could never happen because of my possible problem."

"Well it has! Are you happy?" she asked.

"Am I happy? Yes of course I am happy!"

That Saturday morning Bert wanted to tell the world that he was going to be a father. What would it be - a daughter or a son? He didn't mind what it was, as he and Gwyneth were so excited. That evening after tea Gwyneth sat him down and gave him an order.

"Bertram, now listen to me. I know that you are all excited at the prospect of becoming a father, and as you always go down to the White Hart for a drink on Saturday night you must make me a promise."

Bert nodded obediently.

"Tonight when you go to the White Hart I want you to tell everyone about our good fortune, I am so proud of you."

Tears welled up in Bert's eyes as they embraced. Later that evening, Jack Dawson the manager of Charley Chans Chippy smiled as Bert swayed across the shop floor and rested his elbows on the counter top.

"I guess you've had a good night at the pub, Bert. Bit of a celebration was it?"

"Yes," Bert slurred. "And you will never guess what I am celebrating."

"And I am sure that you are going to tell me all about it," Jack said.

"I," slurred Bert. "Yes I, am going to be a dad!"

"Well good for you Bert. Congratulations! Your chips and curry sauce are on the house Bert, in fact you can have an extra portion of curry sauce on your chips!"

Picking up his portion of curry and chips Bert swayed his way towards the shop doorway. He suddenly stopped, then slowly turning around with a broad smile on his face, he said:

"And Jack, would you like to know what I have got when I get home?"

"No, but I am sure it must be something very special."

"I have got a door key, and a brand new toilet brush!"

"Goodnight Bert, stay safe."

Smile Away

Stress is what we need the least,
Remove it from your mind.
It is such an ugly beast,
Blocking happiness in kind.

Laughter is the medicine,
It's no good being glib.
Display a joyous grin
And tickle someone's rib!

Live a life of humour,
It's good to have a laugh,
Eliminates the trauma,
Though some might think you're daft!

Awaken every morning,
Put on a happy smile.
Troubles they are nothing
For life is not a trial.

Lost

"So this is it! No car, in the middle of who knows where, and not one of you could read a map, even if we had one! And in this wonderful world of technology, the battery has gone dead on our only means of communication, a mobile phone."

"But Dad…"

"Never mind the 'but Dad'. In my younger days we never had all this so-called technology, with all your sat navs and fancy communication systems. We had to rely on the art of navigating by our common instincts to get anywhere."

"But Dad…"

"Are they the only two words you can string together, 'but Dad'? That is the problem with today's generation, they rely too much on their mobile phones and texting, they have lost the art of communication."

"Your mother, who I might say was not the sharpest tool in the box when it came to navigating her way around, was always an absolute treasure whenever we set sail on a journey. Not once did she ever show any signs of mutiny when I decided to choose the route home."

"But Dad, this is car park A, and we want car park C!"

Who Nose

I've often wondered why it chose
For hair to grow from my nose.
When I was young and in my prime,
It didn't seem to have the time.
From being born, it was instead,
Simply growing on my head.
As I grew older hair did grow,
Bodily it did show,
Arms and legs, even toes,
But nothing growing from my nose.
Through my youth I was so proud,
A head of hair, so well endowed.
Combing, preening, mirror gaze,
Young in spirit, happy days.
Years passed by without a care,
And still I had my head of hair.
Until one day my head felt cold,
My hair was thin; I was going bald.
From forehead, skin began to show,
What a horror, oh no!
And so my hair it did recede.
Is there no stopping of this deed?
Massage treatment, but no doubt,
The hair just keeps on dropping out.

Finally, I must accept,
My hair no longer can be kept.
A comb no longer do I use,
Forget the worries and the blues.
I was happy for a while,
Carefree, jolly, with a smile,
Until one day it all went bad,
Someone questioned their Granddad.
Granddaughter studied me up close,
Asked why hair grew from my nose.
I replied, I didn't know,
When on my head it would not grow.
Does one's hair grow downhill
As my nostrils slowly fill?
For at my age I have no fears,
As now it's growing from my ears!

Moving On

DEBBY KNOCKED ON the door of her parents' house, a semi-detached house located in a run-down area of the town. As she stood waiting for a response she admired the new door and windows, which enhanced the appearance of the house in contrast to the other houses in the street. Inwardly she also felt an overwhelming sense of shame. Living only eight miles away, on the other side of town, she had not had any contact with her parents for the last ten years, all because of a tiny disagreement over a money loan which her father had given her.

Her heart sank momentarily as the door opened and her father Harry stood there. A former coal miner from Yorkshire with a no-nonsense approach to life, he gave a look of surprise at seeing her.

"Hello Dad," Debby said nervously, as she wasn't quite sure of the reception she would receive from him after such a long absence.

"Oh, it's you Debby. I suppose tha'd better come in."

My God, thought Debby, he does not change one bit. Here I was all full of apologies, ready to beg forgiveness for the past ten years of lost contact, and what do I get: 'Oh it's you Debby. I suppose tha'd better come in.'

Taking a deep breath, she followed him through into the living room. Apart from him looking older, nothing seemed to have changed about her father. He was a tall gangly figure, still with a good head of hair, but now with a suntanned face since he had retired from working in the coal mines. She couldn't help noticing the quality of the décor and furnishings, a far cry from her last visit when things in the house had begun to get a little threadbare. Reaching the living room, he turned and gave her a hug at the same time kissing her cheek. Tears began to form in her eyes as he released his grip and looked directly into her face.

"Now come on lass, no tears. Just sit theesen dahn," he said motioning her towards a comfy armchair.

"How is Mum?" she asked. "Her health wasn't very good the last time we talked and that was at least ten years ago."

A sudden worried look crossed his face.

"I'm forgetting me manners. Would tha like a cuppa? I should 'ave offered thee one when tha first arrived. I'll go put kettle on," he said as he made his way towards the kitchen.

With her father not responding to her question regarding the health of her mother, Debby began to wonder if she had asked an awkward question. Minutes later he returned with two cups of tea, placing them on a side table along with a plate of biscuits.

"Now lass, how is thee husband Dennis and the kids? Now what was their names? Oh I remember - Alice, Jaime, and Robert."

"Dad, I asked how Mum was."

"I'll bet them kids are right beauties. Tell me, how old are they now?"

"Alice is thirteen, Jamie fourteen, and Robert sixteen!" Debby said irritably.

"Dad, excuse me for getting a little irate," Debby said raising her voice. "But for the third time, where is my Mum, as you have made no mention of her since I arrived?"

As she looked directly at him he lowered his face, his eyes avoiding her gaze and gave a muffled reply: "She's dead."

"What did you say? Did you say that she is dead?"

"Yes," he said quietly.

"I don't believe this! I know we have had our differences for many years', Dad, but to not tell me that my own mother had died, well that certainly takes the biscuit!"

Debby's voice was by now beginning to reach fever pitch.

"And tell me dear father, just when did this event come to fruition?"

"About five years ago," Harry replied.

"Five years ago and you didn't even have the decency to tell me that my own mother had died, and not even an invitation to the funeral! That is disgusting, in fact it is worse than disgusting it is outrageous, you should be damn well ashamed of yourself!! And you call yourself a father!"

"We didn't 'ave a funeral," Harry muttered in reply.

"You didn't have a funeral! Wait a minute, you said 'we'. Who the hell is this 'we'?" Debby yelled.

"It was yer Aunt Emily from Donny."

"Aunt Emily from Doncaster, and tell me father, how did she become part of this conspiracy? And why didn't you have a funeral?"

"Because I spent most of me money looking after yer Ma, I couldn't afford her a proper send off. I even 'ad to give up me part-time job to care for her."

"But if you did not have a funeral where did you bury her?" Debby asked.

A look of embarrassment crossed Harry's face before he gave out a muffled reply, preceded by a false cough.

"In the garden," he said quietly.

"In the garden!!" Debby shrieked.

"Debby, please do not shout so loud, you will alarm the neighbours!"

"Alarm the neighbours! Who gives a damn about your neighbours! How you've got the nerve to sit there and tell me that you buried my mother in the garden! You are worse than Dr Crippen!! God, what next? I suppose you had a celebration afterwards with a firework display to round it off!"

"Well actually, it was on November the fifth," Harry replied. "We thought that would be best time to do the burial when everyone was watching the fireworks, after all it were a sensitive occasion."

"'Sensitive' occasion, Dad, I doubt very much that you even know the meaning of the word! And after my Mum died I suppose that you kept her body in a freezer until November the fifth, just because, as you put it, it was a 'sensitive occasion'."

"Not really," Harry replied. "Because yer Ma died on November the fourth."

Debby opened her mouth as if to speak but nothing came out.

Furrowing his brow Harry asked: "Who's Doctor Crippen?"

Debby pulled out a tissue from her handbag to dab away her tears. For the next few minutes both sat in silence, Debby with tears slowly trickling down her cheeks, Harry with his chin down on his chest too embarrassed to face her.

She was the first to speak: "Where is the bathroom, Dad?"

"Upstairs lass, the first door on tha left."

She made her way from the living room and slowly climbed the stairs. Minutes later she came back, having regained more of her composure. She sat down once again opposite her father, still finding it hard to understand his motives for what he had done.

"Dad, we have to talk. You must explain to me why you did what you did."

"Well lass, the last time we spoke and 'ad that row over the loan, yer Ma, god rest her soul, was taken ill. And as you know, yer Ma 'ad always been the active one around the 'ouse, going out shopping, always on the go, but this illness hit her hard until it made her housebound."

"Didn't you send for a doctor if she was that ill?"

"Tha's got to be joking, yer Ma see a quack! She'd never trust one, so what could I do?"

161

"She began to spend more and more time in bed, and from that moment on I found it very hard looking after her, and that's when it 'appened."

"What happened, Dad?"

"Well her sister, yer Aunt Emily from Donny, who we hadn't spoken to for at least eighteen year, suddenly phoned to ask 'ow we were. I explained how yer Ma was and she offered to come and 'elp, which I can assure you lass, I certainly needed."

"I said to 'er it was very kind of 'er to offer 'elp, but what about 'er husband Stanley," he continued. "Do ye remember Uncle Stanley?"

Debby nodded.

"She said he'd died two year ago, and as they never 'ad any bairns it wouldn't be no problem for her to come 'ere. I was a bit worried like as yer Aunt Emily can be quite bossy. Then two days later she arrived."

"And was she any help, Dad, or was she domineering?" Debby asked.

"She was like an angel, taking charge of everything - the washing, the shopping... In fact, all the local shopkeepers thought she was yer Ma because they looked so alike. And this resemblance would eventually work out to our advantage, because yer poor Ma couldn't get outta bed. Anyway yer Ma, poor lass, she got worse..."

"Dad, just slow down. What did you mean when you said it would work out to your advantage? And who is this 'our', as in 'our advantage', are you referring to Aunt Emily?"

Harry gave a nervous cough and his face began to redden.

"Well lass it were like this, me and yer Aunt Emily by this time 'ad got quite close, and then there were the benefits we 'ad to consider. How else de you think I could afford to fix up this house?"

"Dad, what are you talking about, you and Aunt Emily getting close...?" Debby's voice gradually tailed off. "I don't believe it, are

162

you telling me that you and Aunt Emily had begun to have a relationship while your wife, my mother, was still alive? Have you no shame?!"

"Well we were discreet about it."

"Discreet! The plot thickens. Tell me more, Dad, I am fascinated!" her voice once again reaching fever pitch.

"And I am slightly confused by the 'benefits' you talk about, what benefits?" Debby continued. "Presumably you were in direct receipt of, for want of a better word, 'benefits' from Aunt Emily, but what were these other benefits?"

"Money," Harry replied.

Debby sat open-mouthed.

"Money? Don't tell me, let me guess - you and Aunt Emily formed a team to go around robbing people!" Debby said mockingly.

"No lass, it were easier than that. Let me explain."

"Not very long after yer Aunt Emily arrived and after we 'ad begun to get a bit closer, we discussed our personal circumstances, and she told me that she were not very 'appy living in 'er bungalow in Donny all by 'erself," he continued. I found it very strange her saying that, 'cause many years ago she told me that the bungalow was her dream home. In fact, it were the one place I wished I could afford to live."

Debby sat listening intently as Harry continued.

"Anyway, after a long discussion I agreed she could kip at ours, and she would rent out 'er bungalow to give 'er a steady income."

"And that is where the extra money would come from?" Debby queried.

"No lass, it were better than that."

"Better than that, Dad. How much better?"

"Oh about 200 quid a week."

"Two hundred pounds a week, Dad. How the heck do you fiddle that amount of money without getting caught?"

"Easy really, as me and yer Ma 'ad a joint bank account. Her pension kept getting paid into the account every month, along with 'er other sickness benefits."

"And even after Mum had died?"

"Oh yes," Harry replied confidently. "You see, Debby, it were easy, 'cause I didn't register yer Ma's death, and with yer Aunt Emily acting as if yer Ma were still alive no one would ever be any the wiser."

"But Dad, that is fraud! You could go to jail if they found out."

Harry looked directly into her eyes before giving a broad smile.

"But they never will find out lass, and that is guaranteed."

"And they are still paying into the account, even now?" Debby asked incredulously.

"No lass, not any longer. It stopped about two month ago," Harry replied.

"Nah would tha like to see where thee mother is buried?" Harry said, quickly changing the subject.

Debby followed him as he made his way towards the French windows which looked out on to the rear garden.

"Nah Debby, does tha see that apple tree in t' middle of t' lawn? Well that's where I laid thee Ma to rest, God rest her soul."

"Dad, how could you? How could you!"

Debby sat down on a chair near the French windows, tears once again forming in her eyes. Harry placed a comforting hand on her shoulder.

"I'm sorry lass for what I 'ave done, but at t' time I was a little confused and I didn't set out to cause any upset."

Debby placed her hand on his which was still resting on her shoulder, feeling its comforting warmth.

"If tha wants to go out and sit by t' apple tree lass, I can go and make us another cuppa."

"No that's fine. Dad, I will do that before I go home. I hope I never have to endure another day like this one, ever."

She got up and returned to sit in the armchair.

"And how did Aunt Emily cope with the death of Mum, I guess she was very upset?"

"Yes, she was," Harry replied. "Although she felt the loss of yer Ma when she died, she never grieved that much 'cause when they were nippers they never saw eye to eye."

"Well after yer Ma died, me and yer Aunt Emily gradually settled into the routine of living together," Harry continued. "Then three year' later she suggested we each make out a will, leaving our estates to whoever was the survivor between us. And we also agreed that if she survived me all of my estate would pass on to her, and upon her death all of her assets would pass on to you, Debby, and your family."

He continued, "I thought to mesen that were a pretty good deal like, 'cause as Emily said she had no surviving reli's, therefore with this 'ouse worth about hundred and eighty thou', and along with Aunt Emily's bungalow, it would be a nice inheritance one day for you and the nippers."

"So we went and talked to a solicitor and agreed all t' details before getting everything signed and sealed. Then four week after signing t' wills I booked us on a ten-day Mediterranean cruise. We had a fab time, but until that cruise I never realised how much vino Aunt Emily could neck. She could get down a bottle so quick and still walk in a straight line. She certainly enjoyed being the life and soul of the party."

He was on a roll now: "On t' final night of t' cruise, and when t' ship were about seven hour from Southampton, yer Aunt Emily were once again the life and soul of t' party in t' bar. And as t' bar were closing that night, she boasted to everyone in there that she could balance barefoot on t' top handrail out on t' deck for ten

165

seconds, and could I film her doing it. Once Aunt Emily 'ad made up 'er mind nothing were going to stop 'er, even though I tried to persuade 'er not to do it."

"Dad, I forgot to ask you earlier, how is Aunt Emily?" asked Debby.

"Oh yes, Aunt Emily," he mumbled, ignoring Debby's question. "Well a week after we signed t' wills Aunt Emily were taking 'er morning bath, and a letter arrived addressed to 'er. On the front of t' envelope was t' return address of a solicitor who specialised in writing wills, but not t' solicitor which we 'ad employed to finalise our wills."

"So naturally I were curious. I carefully steamed open t' letter, and it said that documentation that she 'ad requested for leaving all of 'er assets to an animal sanctuary would be ready for signing in about five week."

"Dad, once again, what about Aunt Emily?"

Harry gave another false cough, his right hand rubbing his chin in a fretful motion before answering.

"She's dead," he replied, so quietly it was barely audible.

"Sorry Dad, what did you say?" Debby asked.

"She's dead," Harry repeated, but a little louder this time.

Debby's hands clasped her face: "Dad, what have you done?"

"When Aunt Emily went out to balance on that rail on the cruise ship you pushed her over the side, didn't you?" Debby said. "What a wicked thing to do!"

Tears once again flowed down her face.

"Debby, lass, before tha starts getting all upset listen to what I am going to tell thee."

He took a deep breath before he continued, "That last night on t' cruise ship yer Aunt Emily climbed up onto that top rail on t' deck in front of witnesses, t' other drinkers from t' bar. I 'eld 'er 'and to give 'er some balance, unfortunately our 'ands were wet due to t' spray, she slipped and she were gone, God rest her soul."

"And t' enquiry concluded that it were a tragic accident," he added.

A look of relief spread over Debby's face.

"Oh Dad, please forgive me for what I just said, I am so confused. And after you had registered Aunt Emily's death, didn't people begin to ask you questions about my Mum?"

Harry's face broke into a broad smile.

"Let me put thee in t' picture lass. One thing tha never knew was that Aunt Emily had the same name as thee Ma, and so she was able to use thee Ma's passport."

"I don't understand, Dad, surely it is not possible for sisters to have the same name."

"Well, let me explain lass. Yer Ma were christened Iris, and Aunt Emily were christened Iris Emily, so it weren't Aunt Emily who died at sea it were thee Ma! I should also mention that I 'ave sold this house and will be moving into Aunt Emily's bungalow in Donny next month."

Haircut Sir?

I was busy round the house apace,
When in the mirror I glanced my face.
For a moment I did stare.
How can I improve my hair?

Off to the barbers I should go,
But my money's getting low.
The barber I would give the slip,
For I would give my hair a snip.

Electric clippers borrowed from my lad
Will make me look a youthful dad.
So plug them in, wow do they buzz,
Soon get rid of all this fuzz.

Gently, gently off we go.
Take it easy, nice and slow.
That's not right it isn't level,
Must get rid of that bevel.

Oh my God, what have I done?
I've better hair upon my bum!
What can I do but live in hope,
That I don't look a proper dope.

The door did open; it was my wife.
This is it, now for strife.
She raved at me and gave me stick,
Said I looked a stupid prat.

Off to the barbers to put it right.
God I looked an awful sight!
Talk abated when I walked in.
Was that a snigger or a grin?

The barber looked at me so strange,
Perhaps he thought I had the mange.
He set about and cut the lot,
I no more look a proper clot!

Mirrors I now pass with care,
No longer looking at my hair.
I've passed my youth, I told my lad.
Here are your clippers from your Dad.

Life

(A brief personal expression from the heart of the author)

I was born long ago, the day I don't remember.
As I grew, I was told it was the tenth of December.
Food was short, and clothing too, winters very cold.
Life was tough, so were we, onward being bold.
Comfort I remember, when trousers wore so thin,
My mother sewing patches, to warm my frozen skin.
Father mending shoes, for money we had none,
Being very poor, that's what war had done.
Meals very meagre, for us no bacon or ham,
What I do remember is my love of bread and jam.
Nothing ever wasted, not even dried up bread,
Empty stomachs rumbling, what an awful dread.
My first day off to school, I remembered oh so well.
"Please don't send me there, don't send me I did yell."
Protests were ignored, though I shed some tears,
Just what lay ahead was my greatest fear.
My fear turned to joy as I learned to spell,
Calmness overcame me, panic it did quell.
Discipline was strict, to hand was kept a cane,
From this slim deterrent I was to feel the pain.
Cars were very few, journey's a special treat.
A carefree life we lived, cricket in the street.
Police they had respect, everyone admired,
A dedicated force, so very little crime.

Seasons passed so swiftly, with them I did grow,
A working life did beckon, into I must go.
So began anew, another learning curve,
Sometimes trepidation, hidden amongst the verve.
Then arrived the day, I took upon a wife,
Later came the children, how it changed our life.
Dedication, work, keeping close together,
Sharing all our toils when darkened clouds did gather.
We gave the children love from which they should derive,
Always give and take to gain an honest life.
The children now are married, a family of their own,
Life moves on in earnest, everyone has grown.
Now we've reached our threshold, slower but still bold,
Hair is grey and thinning, gradually getting old.
But memories we'll have to cherish and to keep,
For the day will come when families will weep.

Strings, What Strings?

"ZIP-A-DEE-DOO-DAH..." CHARLEY NEVER got the chance to continue his attempt to sing quietly to himself.

"What are you so damned happy about?" shouted his wife Rosie.

Rosie was Charley's wife, but only by the fact that it had been written on a piece of paper twenty-two years earlier, namely a marriage certificate. Her full name was Rosalind, but she had made it quite clear to Charley that any attempt by him to use it would bring about severe consequences. And Charley was painfully aware of what those consequences could entail! After the honeymoon was over, she became a complete bully and with her physical weight and power Charley was no match for her.

Before their marriage, Charley had visions of it being a life of bliss and slippers by the fireside. And as for having a family, she made it abundantly clear on the honeymoon there wasn't going to be any of that nonsense!

The one thing she really loved though was food. After they married, although she was already a little on the large side, her weight increased further mainly because of her love for junk food. Rosie was never interested in preparing a cooked meal, not even on a weekend, and so Charley had his meals in the staff canteen, and on weekends he was quite content to have a few sandwiches. However, after 22 years of a bullying marriage he had learned how to pull her strings and get away with it.

Charley instantly ceased his singing. Singing had been one of his passions since childhood, and encouraged by his parents he joined a local choir when he was fifteen years of age. One evening a month Rosie would allow Charley out to attend the choir practice.

Today it was a rainy Sunday, a miserable day but with a forecast for improvement later in the morning. Rosie insisted, as she always did every Sunday, that they drove out into the countryside. This was always a welcome break away from their terraced house on the outskirts of Sheffield. But as Rosie had always insisted that she drove the car on Sundays, she religiously went to the same area in the Derbyshire Peak District as they had done for the previous eighteen years. Charley didn't like it where she parked the car, as it was on a slight grassy slope leading to a steep drop onto a series of rocks, and beyond that a near vertical drop of 1,500 feet.

When he first met Rosie she worked on the checkout in a supermarket in Sheffield. Four years after they married she decided they could manage on Charley's wage, and so she decided to stay at home and live a life of idleness. Charley was a general manager at a food distribution warehouse in Sheffield. He had the opportunity for retirement at fifty-five, but without saying anything to Rosie decided against it. Better the devil you know, he thought.

As the car wipers flicked intermittently to clear the wet from the windscreen, Charley allowed himself a faint smile. His other great love in life was gardening. Saturday was his gardening day when Rosie went over to Huddersfield to visit her elderly mother. And when Charley went gardening he was not alone.

Rosie had a younger sister, Elsie. It all began just over three years ago. Elsie's husband Dennis had died suddenly four years earlier. They lived in the next street, where the bottom of Charley's garden met theirs. They had an only son, Philip who was in the armed forces, and so when Dennis died, Elsie began finding it a little difficult taking care of the house and garden.

Charley's garden was just large enough for a medium-sized greenhouse and a small patch of ground which was suitable for growing a few vegetables. And because Rosie never did any cooking he would give these away to friends. But he always longed for the use of a decent potting shed and a larger garden from where he could grow even more produce. After Elsie had gotten over the death of her husband Dennis, she decided to ask Charley if he would be interested in taking over her garden. Charley accepted the offer and he was soon making use of the potting shed in which there was a large bench.

There had never been any serious closeness between Charley and Elsie even though they had always enjoyed each other's company. That was until Charley's fifty-second birthday. Rosie had gone on her usual trip to visit her mother in Huddersfield and Charley was busy in the potting shed in Elsie's garden. He had just completed cleaning and dusting down the bench when Elsie crept in quietly behind him and without a word flung her arms around him.

"Happy Birthday, Charley. I have a present for you, will you accept?"

"From you, Elsie, I will accept anything."

Turning around he fell silent and open-mouthed, for she had unbuttoned her blouse revealing her breasts, and then proceeded to unzip her trousers, letting them fall down around her ankles. She was the complete opposite in size to Rosie, dark-haired and with a slender figure.

Charley was still gaping open-mouthed when Elsie moved forward and began kissing him, at the same time unbuttoning his shirt. Unable to contain a long stored up physical passion, Charley responded to her as they proceeded to make full use of the now clean bench.

Initially, Charley had pangs of guilt about their Saturday meetings, but he gradually realised that after a loveless marriage he had finally found some happiness in his life, and his inner feelings for Elsie went far beyond just their physical relationship. Charley didn't reveal his feelings to Elsie, but somehow she felt that he was afraid to admit his love for her.

Two months earlier she had suggested that, perhaps, Charley should consider moving in with her. Charley, however, explained that when he made his vows (till death do us part) he would stick to them, even though Elsie's offer was very tempting. Elsie accepted this and promised him his decision would not change their relationship.

Then last week the news arrived that Charley had been dreading. Rosie's mother was seriously ill and was not expected to live beyond the next three weeks.

Charley was shaken out of his thoughts as the car hit a pothole in the narrow track that led up to where they were going to park, passing a notice which advised that it was not safe for motor vehicles to proceed any further. It also added that it was unsafe to park any cars on the grassy slope to the left of the track. Typically, this suggestion only inflamed Rosie's defiance even more. Who were they to tell her where she could or could not park her car. Then suddenly the sun broke through the cloud.

"Stop, please stop," Charley said.

"What do you mean stop?!" Rosie yelled. "Who are you to tell me to stop? Who's driving this car, me or you?"

"I was just going to say that you have driven past the entrance to where you need to park the car, and you will need to reverse to get into there," Charley replied nervously.

"Perhaps I should get out to check the grass and make sure that it is not too slippery to safely park the car," He added.

"Of course I will have to reverse into there. What do you expect me to do, carry the damn thing?!" Rosie said angrily. "And as for the condition of the grass I will decide on its condition not you! Now if you must get out, get out now!"

By now Rosie's face was red with rage. Charley duly obliged by getting out of the car. He then walked back and through the gateway into the field and took up a position of about 30 feet from where the edge of the field fell away down the steep drop. This, he thought, should be the safe stopping point for Rosie to park the car.

The car's rear wheels spun in reverse flinging out pieces of gravel as it tried to get a grip on the wet surface. Shooting back into the field, Rosie then slammed it hard into forward gear, spinning its wheels and racing towards where Charley was standing. Charley stepped quickly to his left as the car, with its brakes full on and wheels locked, sped past. As the car slid past Charley, Rosie's face contained a total look of disbelief and horror. Charley's gaze followed the descent of the car as it hit the rocks down the slope, the final bounce sending it into a somersault before it disappeared.

For a brief moment Charley stood silent. Then, giving a half smile of sadness and relief, he quietly mouthed the words: "No more strings."

With arms outstretched to give his lungs their full capacity he sang one of his favourite songs, which he had first heard sung by Sarah Brightman, 'Time To, Say Goodbye.'

Face the Cream
(or was it Cream the Face)

Time it comes and time it goes,
Wrinkles come but stay on show.
Every day they are in place,
Slowly spreading across my face.
Some they say are laughter lines,
I'm afraid it's the sign of the times.

When I was young and in my prime
My skin required little time.
But as the years went ticking by,
Skin retreated, getting dry.
What could I do? I did despair,
Me so wrinkly, husband no hair.

Then one day I did decide,
These wrinkles I must surely hide.
Then by chance our chemist shop
Had on offer, Wrinkle Stop.
Sales staff hatched a wicked plot
As I went and bought the lot.

Then facing the mirror, I did dream
As I slapped on loads of cream,
Of smooth skin there'd be no doubt,
Wrinkles gone, with joy I'd shout!
Every day I did apply
Onto my skin now not dry.

But looking closely as I dare
The blasted wrinkles are still there!
Of Wrinkle Stop I'd used the lot,
Went and bought another pot.
Puffed my cheeks, forehead pulled taut,
Now I'm getting very fraught.

But the wrinkles still appear,
I won't be beaten, that is clear.
This cream's not doing what it was meant,
My husband's suggestion - use cement!
I try to fill in every crack,
But more it looks like a railway track.

Then desperation leads to dither.
Should I use a different mirror?
So give a smile what you can't appose,
I'll never again be a springtime rose!

About the Author

John Worthington was born in the parish of Brimington, located on the outskirts of Chesterfield, Derbyshire in 1939.

He worked for an engineering company in the Chesterfield area, where he qualified as a mechanical maintenance fitter.

In his late twenties he emigrated with his family to Canada, where he was employed by the Canadian National Railways at their Edmonton workshops in the province of Alberta.

From there he went on to work as an oil rig mechanic for various oil drilling companies operating in Algeria, Iran, Indonesia and Nigeria.

He now resides in the county of Lincolnshire.